Death at the
Mrs Capper's
David W Robinson

© David W Robinson 2023

Edited by Maureen Vincent-Northam
Cover Design Rhys Vincent-Northam

Prologue

Hello and welcome to Christine Capper's Comings and Goings, your weekly video blog of what's been happening in Haxford, brought to you this week by Haxford Hand Car Wash. If your wheels are a mess, bring them to us and we'll clean them for less.

As most of you know, Dennis and I have been together almost thirty years, we don't argue much (not if he knows what's good for him, we don't) but inevitably after so many years there are those occasions when we fall out, usually early in the year when the dark winter nights and short days get to us, and so it was with the one I'm about to divulge.

Like all our disagreements, it started with a couple of trivial items, and mushroomed from there.

The Incident, our name for that terrible evening when two thugs beat Dennis half to death, had cost us a lot in terms of distress and money, but by the beginning of the year, Dennis was back at work full-time, so money was less of an issue. That's when I decided, the kitchen needed redecorating. It had nothing to do with subsequent events, which comprised the second of the trivial items, and although the case in question did not materialise until the summer, the catalyst, in other words, the initial exchange which indirectly led me to the case, happened before our niece's wedding in Cambridge, and before the Prater affair (both of which helped defer the kitchen redecoration).

So before we look at the events of midsummer, let me take you back to a Sunday morning in late January when I dragged Dennis out of bed so I could put clean linen on.

Chapter One

"You want the kitchen doing up?"

Dennis's amazement made it sound as if I'd suggested some kind of obscene act to be performed on the town hall steps. A quick glance around before concentrating on him once again, confirmed the need for redecoration. At least, it did to me, even if Dennis didn't get the silent message.

"Look at the state of the place. It needs a coat of paint, and the wallpaper behind the cooker needs replacing. You can't do just that little bit. You've gotta do the whole thing."

"Yeah, but it's finding time. Crikey, I had enough time off work last year, thanks to those clowns who beat me up. I'm up to my eyes in it at work, and I don't see—"

"To be honest, Dennis, I was thinking of bringing a professional decorator in."

More shock emanating from him. "Do you know how much that'll cost?"

I shrugged. "A couple of hundred pounds. It's not like we can't afford it."

"It'll be nearer a grand, and you're wrong. No way can we afford it. Have you seen the way the price of gas and electric are going up?"

Even if I hadn't, Dennis's regular checking the

smart meter would have educated me. He kept a careful eye on both accounts and whined constantly about the cost, particularly when I switched on the central heating.

"I'm not interested, Dennis. I want a professional decorator in here to do the kitchen up. Now who should I call? Come on. You're the man who knows everyone in Haxford. You service most of their cars. Who's best?"

It was with a considerable sulk that he said, "I'll talk to Snoddy."

"Snoddy?"

"Barry Snodgrass. He does better than a fair to middling job, and he won't bankrupt us."

I smiled in triumph. "I can leave it in your capable hands then."

We left it at that, but it was about the same time when the second trivial item I mentioned earlier raised its ugly head. This was a bitterly cold weekend in January with a layer of snow and ice on the pavements, when I protested, "I need heating in that bedroom, Dennis. It's freezing when I go to bed." It was all right for him. I usually went to bed first and by the time he came along, I'd warmed the bed up for him.

"There are other ways of keeping warm," he retorted.

"If you're thinking what I think you're thinking you can forget it."

"I'm not talking about that," he interrupted, his ears turning bright red, which confirmed my theory that he was thinking what I thought he was thinking. On the other hand, he did deny it, so…

"What are talking about then?" I demanded, bringing my focus to bear on the debate.

"You don't warm the room, you warm the bed. You use a hot water bottle." He gave me his smuggest smile. One that suggested he had just invented solar powered, heated beds.

"Hot water bottle?" Even to me, my voice sounded as if I'd just heard him mention something obscene like sacrificing a chicken and sleeping in the fresh, warm blood. "No one's used hot water bottles since my grandma's day."

"No, but I bet they'll be starting again what with the way the price of gas keeps going up. And it's not like it's illegal. And I'm sure we've got at least one somewhere in the house, and if not, we can get them for a fiver apiece. Fill them out of the kettle, and—"

"The moment you put one of your laser sharpened toenails through one, we'll end up with a wet bed. I am not using hot water bottles."

"My toenails are not that sharp."

"I could slice the Sunday roast with them." I shuddered at the thought of such an unhygienic prospect.

The argument could have gone on for days had I not taken executive action that very morning. I went out and paid thirty pounds for an electric underblanket from the homewares department of CutCost. I couldn't find king size, so I bought double instead. Well, I thought it would be fine for warming the centre of the mattress, which was really the only bit we needed to heat.

I was right. From the very first night I noticed the difference. Better than that, it only cost pennies to run. It was so cheap on electricity that we hardly noticed the difference in our bills, although Dennis certainly remarked on the reduction in the amount of gas we burned.

It fitted on top of the mattress and was held in place by long, elasticated straps which went round the mattress side to side, and because it was a double, not a king-size, there was a gap of about four inches on either side of the bed. Over the next week or two, I noticed that I had to move closer to the middle of the bed to get any benefit from it, and I couldn't understand why. When I stripped the bed and checked, it had sneaked over right to the edge of Dennis's side.

I realised right away that an electric blanket, no matter how technically advanced, could not sneak of its own accord. Dennis had been reaching under the fitted sheet to pull it his way.

On a chilly Sunday morning during the last days of January, I challenged him, and he denied it. "It's nowt to do wi' me."

"Then how has it happened?"

With the bed completely stripped, only the sparse underblanket looking forlorn in the middle of the mattress, Dennis put on his thoughtful look and walked round the bed. It was the kind of face he put on for customers when he walked round their vehicles, assessing potential problems and looking for ways and means to jack up the bill.

Eventually, he said, "It's your side of the bed. The mattress is sagging in the middle of that edge."

I was too old a hand to be fooled by that. When all was said and done, we'd had that mattress a fair while so it was bound to get misshapen. I took him to task again. "And how would that explain the blanket creeping to your side of the bed?"

"The elastic straps." He walked to my side and pressed down on the mattress. "See, when you compress it on your side, you ease the tension on that side of the elastic straps, but because they're anchored at the other side, they tend to pull it my way."

What I knew about the technology of six-foot, elastic straps you could write on a post-it note and still leave room for a copyright statement. Even so, Dennis's explanation didn't sound right.

"The mattress sags on your side, too."

"Yeah, but I've always been heavier than you. So that was accommodated when you first strapped the blanket to the mattress. It's your side that's sagged since we bought it. You've put weight on."

I curbed the immediate inclination to throw something at him. The only things to hand were a range of perfume bottles, and I'd paid a fortune for most of them. "Dennis, do you remember when those two thugs beat you up during last May's election campaign?"

He grunted. "Will I ever forget?"

"That was nothing at the side of what I'll do if you accuse me of putting on weight again."

"But you have," he protested.

"A couple of pounds. Nothing to write home about."

"Yeah, well, from where I'm stood it's more like half a stone."

I knew perfectly well that it was more than half a

stone. All the same, I warned him, "If you don't shut up, you won't be standing there much longer. You'll be on your way to A&E."

I stood back looking at the bed. We'd only had the base for about three years. A split divan, four drawer affair, it was still strong, almost as good as it was when we bought it.

The mattress was another story. Working from memory, I estimated we'd had it for about five or six years. When I checked later, I discovered we'd actually had it for ten years, and I was sure I'd read somewhere that you should change your mattress every three years.

That decided me. "We'll have to get a new mattress."

If there was one thing guaranteed to distract Dennis's mind from my weight, elastic straps, the price of gas, and motor vehicle engineering, it was the thought of spending even more money. "A new…new… mattress. Do you know how much they cost?"

"They're not that expensive. Come on. Let's get a bit of breakfast and we can go down to Sleepy-Byes."

Sleepy-Byes was one of the businesses renting most of one floor in Haxford Mill, where Dennis and his partners also had their premises.

"I can't go to Sleepy-Byes. I work in that mill. If anyone sees me, I'll never live it down."

"If you don't get a move on, you'll be sleeping at the workshop for the foreseeable future. No more arguments. Breakfast and we're going."

When Dennis said he worked in that mill, he was half right. He and his partners rented two large workshops on the ground floor around the canal side of the mill. In theory then, there was no reason why anyone from Sleepy-Byes would know him.

In theory.

In practice, just about everyone in Haxford Mill knew him. He serviced and repaired most of their cars and he was a regular customer at Sandra's Snacky on the third floor. When we emerged from the service lift on the second floor, a number of people called out to him, most of them passing jocular comments on his lack of a boiler suit and spanners.

If that was embarrassing for him, matters got worse when we approached one of the salespeople, a woman by the name of Sylvia (according to her nametag). A tall and leggy, forty-something blonde, most of her spindly limbs showing beneath the hem of a skirt that was at least six inches and twenty years too short for her, she had a haughty Harrods-ish air about her, spelled out by the way she referred to Dennis as 'sir', and me as 'modom'.

From the moment she opened her mouth and spoke, she got on my nerves. If I was annoyed with Dennis for his references to my weight, it was nothing compared to the way I felt about her.

As it turned out, Dennis was right. Not about never being able to live down his visit to the mill on a Sunday, but about the price of beds and mattresses. I'm sure we didn't pay that for our entire set of bedroom furniture: bed, two wardrobes, dresser and its seat, and a couple of chests of drawers.

A big part of the problem was that 'modom's servant' wasn't listening properly. We were looking for a mattress and she was trying to sell us a bed. And for the price of these beds, I'm sure I could have had a week in Benidorm. According to Dennis, he didn't pay that much for his precious Morris Marina. That wasn't saying much, mind. He bought the car in bits from scrap yards and rebuilt it from scratch. All up, I estimated it cost him less than four hundred pounds. For the price of one of Sleepy-Byes' beds, he could have bought a small fleet of such wrecks.

Even when I protested, the stupid woman didn't listen and focussed instead on Dennis. "Perhaps sir would like to test the bed?"

At this point, she was so far up my nose she was picking my brains and I decided it was time to fight back.

"No, love. Dennis and I are far too old. Tell you what though, if you get one of your strapping young lads from the warehouse we can watch you and him giving the bed a run for its money."

She gawped, Dennis blushed.

There was a time when I would never have dared to say anything so outrageous. Not even in fun. But over a year of working for Radio Haxford had increased my confidence to the point where I could go over the top without blushing, and that was an example.

And it worked. It shut the saleswoman's mouth and seized up her brain to the stage where I could at last get her to listen to me.

"We don't want a bed. We want a mattress. Now if you'd be so kind as to show us the mattresses, perhaps we'll make some progress."

It was an equally pointless exercise. As Dennis

predicted, the prices were just as extreme as my crass comment, and I point blank refused to negotiate with her. On the desperation line, determined to make a few coppers in commission, she suggested a mattress topper.

"It's like giving your mattress a new lease of life, Modom," she urged, and I fell for it. Fifty pounds for a topper.

Dennis did little but grumble and things would only go further downhill when we fitted the topper. Like the underblanket, it was held in place by elasticated straps, but in this instance, it covered the entire mattress. When that was set up, the underblanket came next. So far, so good. Then we tried the fitted sheet and it wouldn't. Fit, I mean. The topper raised the depth of the mattress by another inch or more and the sheet simply would not stretch that far.

"You need some strength, woman," Dennis said and gripped the stretch corner of the sheet. Like the mattress, we had had it a long time and I knew it was wearing a little thin. It was left to my husband to demonstrate just how thin. While I sat on the sheet on the opposite side to ensure it didn't move when he pulled on it, he gave the corner a good tug and the next thing I heard was a tearing sound. I looked over my shoulder to see the bottom corner coming apart from the rest of the sheet.

"Oops."

My temper got the better of me. "Oops? You've just ripped my best sheet apart and all you can say is oops?"

"Best sheet?"

"I paid ten pounds for that sheet and its pillowcases."

"Aye. About fifteen years ago."

"Twelve, actually. Right. That's it. In the car. Let's get to CutCost before they shut."

"CutCost?"

"For new sheets. Move it."

They cost me a shade over twenty pounds, and Dennis made his feelings plain.

"Seventy quid. You've spent seventy quid today. We could have bought fourteen hot water bottles for that price and covered the entire bed. And it's all because you're overweight. Why don't you get some of that lard off?"

The row went on until early evening when he immersed himself in repeats of *Bangers & Cash* and I sulked in the conservatory.

Chapter Two

I'd never heard of Barry Snodgrass, but Dennis told me that the poor man was snowed under with work, and he would get to us as soon as he could. Inevitably, when he did, it clashed with my niece Jocelyn's wedding, and we had to be in Cambridge for the weekend.

Then he was busy, busy, busy and couldn't fit us in, so the next time we heard, was a few days before Dennis and I were scheduled to shoot off to Lanzarote for a much needed holiday, and obviously, we couldn't fit him in. I recall thinking as we climbed on the plane at Manchester airport that the way things were going, my kitchen was unlikely to be redecorated this side of Christmas.

This was soon after the successful outcome of the Prater case, and we enjoyed a fabulous week of unbroken sunshine and scorching temperatures in Puerto del Carmen. Seven days of lazing around the pool, dragging Dennis to the Biosfera Shopping Mall and forcing him to open his wallet, and enjoying good food and drink while we watched evening entertainment in various bars. I even forgot about the kitchen.

One thing I'll say for the Canary Islands; they made Dennis almost human. We spent our honeymoon in the same hotel and then, as now, he enjoyed nothing more than sleeping off the beer by the poolside, and when we were out and about, he took pictures of the cars, buses and lorries flitting about the place. But that was Dennis. Even on holiday, he ignored the scenery and indulged his passion for motor vehicles.

Throughout the week we only fell out once, and that was on the Wednesday when I decided to enjoy a swim in the pool one afternoon. I hadn't visited Haxford public baths in years, but with the sun beating down from a pure blue, cloudless sky, the temperature rising, sweat forming on my brow, the temptation proved too great. I took off my thin poolside wrap and made my way to the water's edge where I dipped my toe in and promptly pulled it back out again. That water was freezing.

It wasn't, obviously, but it took me some time to pluck up the courage to walk into the water a few inches at a time. Children and a few young adults were throwing themselves freely in, and I envied them. I was sure the shock would kill me. After several minutes, by which time the water was just above my knees, I threw caution to the wind and sat down... and promptly stood up again. Good lord. Had they pushed the water through a refrigerator before dropping it into the pool?

Eventually, I immersed myself, making sure to keep my hair above water (I'd paid a fortune to have it done at Sonya's Unisex on the High Street before we left home) I pulled through three leisurely circuits of the pool's perimeter before getting out again, and that's when Dennis said it.

Lowering his cheap, fake Ray Bans, he looked me up and down. "I suppose you're gonna tell me your swimsuit's shrunk."

"Don't be daft. What use is a swimsuit that shrinks in the wash?"

"Well, it looks a bit tight. Don't you think it's time you bought a bigger size?"

I scowled. "Don't start that again. I had enough of your insinuations in January."

"I'm only telling it like it is. You've put weight on."

I scanned his flat tummy. Flat, true, with a hint of flab. That was a consequence of months of rest after The Incident. "That's rich coming from a chipaholic."

He frowned. "What's a chipaholic?"

"Like a chocaholic but addicted to chips."

"I am not a hipacholic."

"No? Why is it the kitchen needs decorating? Who was it who scorched the wallpaper behind the cooker when he let the chip pan catch fire?"

"I'm not talking about the kitchen. I'm talking about you, and all I'm saying is—"

"You're signing your death warrant. I should shut up while you're ahead."

He was, of course, perfectly correct. I was eight or nine pounds heavier than before last Christmas, but I wouldn't thank him for pointing it out. Besides, we were on holiday. Who cares about diets on holiday? I'd soon lose it when I got home.

And with that, I forgot all about the incident (and the weight) until we attended Craig Wharrier's wedding a few weeks later.

A week in sun-kissed Lanzarote, hardly prepared us for the appalling weather on our in return. Thunderstorms, showers, intermittent sunshine followed by more and more rain, a back garden that was growing far too fast for us to keep up with, and generally speaking, temperatures that were more reminiscent of October than June.

And so it was on the day of Craig Wharrier's wedding. The eldest son of Tony and Val Wharrier, he and Louise, his partner of several years, postponed the wedding by almost a year thanks to the same, scandalous increases in energy charges Dennis complained about so consistently. Like any properly trained woman, Louise must have nagged the pants off him, and in mid-June, they finally tied the knot at Haxford Register Office (or Register Toffees to hear Dennis) followed by a huge thrash at Haxford Social and Working Men's Club.

Tony Wharrier and Dennis were old, old friends, going all the way back to their respective apprenticeships at Addison's, once the largest auto repair company in Haxford. Thanks to his surname, Tony was known affectionately as Geronimo. He specialised in bodywork while Dennis was more the king of the spanners (his description not mine) and when Addison's went under, they founded their own company, Haxford Fixers. From the outset, they were inundated with work and before long, they were joined by another old friend, Lester Grimes, a general electrical whizz kid (household appliances, and auto-electrics) known by the soubriquet, Grimy. It was appropriate. Soap and water and Lester rarely got together. After The Incident, when Dennis was laid off for months, they took on another ex-Addison's mechanic, Greg Vetch, these days known as Herriot because his surname sounded like 'vet'. He was a spanner man like Dennis, and he did such a good job during the months Dennis was absent or could only deal with admin, that they made him a partner in the business.

All four were present at Craig and Louise's wedding. Well, let's face it, Tony had to be, didn't he? I mean it would look odd if the groom's father didn't turn up, wouldn't it? In Haxford, if the groom's father was not present, there was an automatic assumption that the mother did not know who the father was. Either that or he was in prison. Or both.

After the buffet reception and the short speeches were over, it proved a lively, enjoyable afternoon and evening... until Val and I got talking.

She and I were old friends. Well, put it this way; I'd known her for a long time but we only really became friends when we were jointly involved in the Stocker murders. I don't mean we did the murders, but Val roped me into it and I investigated.

A bulky blonde, by which I don't mean fat, but well built, she was some kind of freelance proofreader-stroke-editor for authors who liked to self-publish their work, and she often hinted that she made more than a cheese and tomato sandwich out of the job. From that angle, she was in a similar position to me. Our respective husbands made excellent weekly wages from Haxford Fixers, topped up with a quarterly dividend, and whatever money Val and I earned was more of a bonus than a obviously had more than me because she laughed aloud. "It's a slimming group, Chrissy. Losers as in losing weight." She patted her chunky thighs. "Couldn't stand the sight of myself in a swimsuit in Spain, so when we got back, I decided I need to shed a few pounds."

Pounds? Stones would be nearer the mark. For the sake of peace and quiet I didn't mention the contretemps between Dennis and me at the Lanzarote poolside, or my reflection in the wardrobe mirror of our room, but it all sprang to mind the moment she mentioned the image of herself in a swimsuit. I talked Dennis down, yes, but I knew I'd put on some weight. Even so, I had to suppress a shudder at the thought of Val's prop-forward body clad in nothing but a bikini.

"Anyway, I joined them a month ago," she was saying. "Georgie's a few years older than me, but I've known her for quite some time. I edited a book she'd written, I knew she was into diet and weight loss and stuff like that, so I joined the Losers Club. I'm doing okay. Nearly four weeks now, and I've lost about five pounds."

I had to take her word for it. If she'd lost five pounds, I don't know which area of her vast body she'd lost them from.

She cast an eye over me. "No offence, Chrissy, but you look as if you could do with shedding a little weight."

No offence? NO OFFENCE? Many more comments like that, and I'd soon show her how to lose a good few pounds in the split second it would take to cut off her head.

she was talking about before she asked the question.

Relieved to be back in familiar territory, I agreed that I was.

"Only I thought you'd packed it in for your work on Radio Haxford."

It was an old tale. Eric Reitman, the producer at Radio Haxford asked me to drop my PI licence when he offered me Christine Capper's Mystery Hour. Events at Christmas Manor, and later in both Cambridge and Haxford, all followed by the Prater case, persuaded me otherwise, and in fact it was the mystery hour and my lost friends programmes which I dropped, to take up the Christine Capper Interview instead. It was much more my kind of thing, and if the rumours were true, the two interviews I'd done so far had been greeted favourably by the audience.

I explained this to Val and she tutted. "Trust Tony to get the tale wrong."

"He probably got it from Dennis, so it won't be all Tony's fault. Dennis doesn't listen to me, and in truth he'd love me to give up everything. Then he could really complain about the gas and electricity bills. Anyway, why were you asking? Do you need a private eye?"

"Not me, but a friend, only I'm not sure she could afford you. It's Georgie Tibbett. She runs the Haxford Losers Club, and I'm a member."

At that stage, I'd already had a few Bacardis, and I don't know how I kept myself from laughing. "Haxford Losers Club? Curious name for a social group. I wouldn't have thought you'd be a member. You're hardly a loser, are you?"

I don't know what Val was drinking, but she'd

"Worry? Understatement. He's obsessed with the smart meter. He watches the numbers going up, shakes his head, and says, 'it can't go on'. I think it's hitting the business, too, isn't it?"

"According to Tony, for all the extra work they've taken on with Greg, this next quarter's divi will be a less than it has been. He says their electricity bill has just about tripled. And the council have jacked the rents up by close on ten percent."

"Tell me about it. I've been waiting for my kitchen tarting up for the last six months, and I still haven't seen this decorator Dennis has supposedly talked to. Barry Snodgrass. Have you heard of him?"

Val nodded. "He's good, Chrissy. He'll do you a cracking job, and he won't charge the earth." Determined to change the subject, she asked, "Did you have a good time in Lanzarote?"

"Brilliant, thanks. How was Fuengirola?"

"Marvellous."

From there she proceeded to give me a blow by blow account of a one week break on the Costa del Sol. She began with the moment they boarded the plane at Manchester and ended the moment they got off the plane at Manchester on the way back. Many years had passed since Dennis and I visited that part of Spain, but by the time Val was through, I felt like I'd been there in mid-May with her and Tony.

What was curious was the conclusion to her detailed account. She changed the subject again. "Are you still working as a private eye?"

I couldn't work out quite how my work as a private investigator fitted in with her analysis of the price of clothing in Southern Spain, which is what necessity, although I would argue that I made a considerable amount of money from my efforts as a private investigator and a radio presenter... But I wasn't sure whether I made as much as her.

She was a big girl. Blessed with legs so chunky, anyone could be forgiven for thinking they'd last seen them in the scrum during a six nations rugby match, and she had a large bottom to go with them. Her bosom was perfectly in tune with her lower half, and I always felt that if my top set was that big, I'd need extensions on the car's pedals, because I'd have to sit further back from the steering wheel.

And yet, she was not unlovely. Indeed, she was quite a good-looking woman. It's just that there was a bit too much of her. She had a shower of blonde-ish hair, a smooth, seductive voice, and a warm smile of welcome on her small mouth, but that smile could turn to a come and get me laugh when she was amused by something.

Around nine o'clock in the evening, some kind of argument developed between the Wharriers' youngest son, Rod, and another young man. Lester Grimes, half-drunk by this time, tried to intervene, and it looked as if a full-blown fight was about to develop when Dennis, Tony, and Greg went over to ensure peace reigned.

Keeping out of the way, frowning on the half a dozen souls arguing by the door, Val came to sit with me, shaking her head. "Men. Who'd have 'em?"

"Women like you and me, Val," I said with a cynical smile. "Are you keeping well?"

"Aside from the size of the gas and electricity bill, yes. Does Dennis worry about it?"

I controlled my irritation. I could always take it out on Dennis later. "I'm fine as I am, thank you. Now what about this Georgie Tibbett?"

"There's another slimming club in Haxford. Haxford (not so) Heavies. Run by a woman named Karen Dawkins. Georgie reckons Dawkins has been pinching her members, and to be fair, Dawkins is always slagging Georgie and her club off."

I shook my head. "It's not illegal, Val. If Georgie's members decide they're better off with this Dawkins woman, then there's not much Georgie can do about it. As for slagging Georgie and her members off, the only thing I can say about that is, Georgie should give Dawkins tit-for-tat." I sighed. "There was a time, a long time ago, when companies would never even mention their competitors, but these days, it's quite common to put out veiled insults against one another." I took another sip of Bacardi. "How serious is it?"

Val shrugged her quarterback shoulders. "All I can tell you is that Georgie certainly gets steamed up over it. Any chance you could come and have a word with her? As a favour to me?"

I remembered that after the Stocker case, I never did get paid. Not Val's fault, of course, but it made me wary. Having said that, I didn't have a great deal to do with my time right then. I had no cases, and my work for Radio Haxford took no more than half a day a week. One and a half when I had to record an interview.

"When's the next meeting?"

"Half past seven, Tuesday night. The Haxford Health Spa. You don't have to be a member of the spa, and I'm not suggesting you become a member of Haxford Losers Club, or anything like that because I'll introduce you. You might have to hang around until, say, nine o'clock before you can get a word with her, but I'll smooth the way, I'm sure she'd welcome your advice.

I finally relented. "All right. I'll be there on Tuesday night."

Chapter Three

There was a time when Tuesday and Wednesday were the worst days of the week for me. On Tuesday, I had to be at the Radio Haxford Studios for half past ten in order to deliver my agony aunt slot at eleven o'clock, in the middle of Reggie Monk's morning show. I was usually out of the studio by half past eleven, after which I invariably called at Terry's Tea Bar in the market hall for a cup of tea and a toasted teacake. I was usually home by half past twelve, but the day's work didn't end there. I had to spend the afternoon drafting out another of my mystery tales for delivery during the recording of Christine Capper's Mystery Hour.

That was history. The mystery hour turned into what we seasoned presenters (I'd been doing it over a year and as far as I was concerned I was out of my broadcasting nappies) a turkey and it was dropped in May, which freed Wednesdays up for me. That was largely on the back of the Prater case (no I'm not going into detail) and in its place came the Christine Capper Interview.

These days it was mostly Tuesday which saw me under pressure. The Christine Capper Interview went out once a fortnight and they were recorded wherever the subject felt most comfortable. Since its debut a month previously, we'd only done two and they were recorded in the subjects' homes, but when signing the contract, I had agreed that if necessary, we could deal with it in my conservatory.

That had always presented problems when we were recording the mystery hour. The amount of equipment they brought with them included a soundproof booth which had to be assembled in the conservatory and later dismantled. Then there was a mass of electrical and electronic equipment to put together. Add to that the noise of the generators running all day (no way could I afford to let them use my electricity) and it brought serial complaints from my neighbours.

I took the complaints on the chin. I didn't notice those same neighbours complaining when a news team arrived from TVYK to interview me after the outcome of the Prater case. They asked several of my neighbours what it was like living next door to a minor celebrity. They were all smiles at the thought of a ten-second appearance on the local news.

I didn't thank the TV company for their description of me. Celebrity I was not (although did I become close to behaving like one during the Prater investigation).

Once again, all that was history and these days it was only Tuesday which would find me in a brisk mood.

Three days after Craig Wharrier's wedding Dennis ignited my darker side when he said, "So, you decided to listen to me after all?"

We always took breakfast together on Tuesday. Unless I was involved in a case, I lazed the morning away in bed most of the week, but I needed to be up early on Tuesday so I could get to the Radio Haxford studio in plenty of time.

Dennis's comment, delivered as we sat at the kitchen table, posed a slight puzzle, but I had an idea what he was getting at. I'd warned him on Monday that I would be at Haxford Losers Club on Tuesday evening, but it was practically certain he wasn't listening, and if I was right, his words were the start of an irritated exchange.

I dived straight in. "Listening is more than you do when I'm speaking. What are you talking about?"

"You're going to that slimming club tonight, aren't you? I told you in January, when you were faffing about with the electric blanket, that you needed to get some pounds off, and I said it again in Lanzagrotty when you went swimming."

As I suspected. "Do you have a camp bed at Haxford Fixers?"

He frowned. "No. Why would we need one? We don't have anyone there of a night."

"Many more comments like that and you will have. It'll be you and you'll need the camp bed to sleep on. What did I just say about listening to me, Dennis? Yes, I told you last night that I'm going to Haxford Losers Club tonight, but I also told you I'm not joining them. The woman has some problems, and Val Wharrier asked me if I could advise her."

Having dispensed with his cornflakes, he pushed the empty dish aside. "She needs advice on losing weight? If she needs that kind of advice, what's she doing running a slimming club in the first place? And why would she ask you, cos let's face it…"

"Enough." Having cut him off, I clenched my fists and silently counted to five. "Do us both a favour, and go to work. If you sit here much longer, I swear blind I'll swing for you."

He ignored the threat and stood up, but before he could leave, my mobile rang and it was Barry Snodgrass.

I put a light spring in my voice. "Good morning, Mr Snodgrass. And how are you today?"

"Fine thanks, Mrs C, and I do wish you'd call me Snoddy. Everyone else does. Anyroad up, is there any chance I can get to see you today, get the job costed and stuff?"

"It could be troublesome. I'm on Radio Haxford at eleven o'clock, and I have an appointment this evening."

Alongside me Dennis was frantically waving his hands and shaking his head in a brace of gestures which said, 'forget it'.

"Tomorrow would be better," I told Snodgrass.

"Great. Morning or afternoon?"

With Georgie Tibbett in mind and the need for some rest the following morning, I said, "Afternoon would be better."

"Three-ish?"

"Call it a date."

I ended the call and looked at my husband. "He'll be here tomorrow at three. Now what are you flapping about, Dennis?"

"If I'm not here, he'll charge you for painting the Forth Bridge and then some."

"I am not stupid."

"No, but you don't know what he's talking about.

I do." He made ready to leave again. "I'll have to make sure I'm here tomorrow. For now, will you be here when I get home tonight, or will you already be on your way?"

"I'll be leaving at about seven o'clock. If you're later than that, your dinner will be in the oven. Pass any more snide remarks on my weight and my inability to handle tradesmen and your dinner will be in the cat."

A couple of minutes later, he left for work, and I made for the shower in order to get ready for my agony aunt slot.

***

Working for the station was fun in many ways, but the Tuesday morning agony aunt spot subjected me to one of the worst experiences I had to face every week. Sharing a tiny studio with the morning anchor, Reggie Monk, complete with body odour and halitosis. He'd been a part of Radio Haxford since its launch, about ten years or so ago, and I was surprised that no one had ever dropped a hint to him. He needed to make more use of deodorant sprays, or maybe take a shower more often, and he could do with seeing a dentist.

One thing you couldn't argue with was his popularity. The station's catchment ran to about 15,000 listeners, and Reggie's four-hour stint pulled in the largest audience. That was down to his eclectic choice of music; anything from 30s & 40s swing, to 40s and 50s mood music, to rock 'n' roll, to punk, to post punk, modern pop, and a fair selection from the 60s and 70s.

He was all right, Reggie, but he had this appalling fake laugh which he put out at regular intervals during his show. His 'ha-ha-ha' wasn't restricted to his radio output either. If you got into conversation with him, he used it regularly, especially when he said something that he thought was funny. On a score of one to ten I would rate him at about minus one as a comedian, but you couldn't fault him as a DJ.

Reggie aside, my agony aunt slot was easy. It was a phone in session which ran for about fifteen minutes, and all I had to do was answer questions put by the callers. And I didn't really answer them. The team did all the research, and the answers appeared on a little tablet set in front of me. Although I wasn't on air until eleven, it was incumbent upon me to be at the studio for half past ten for a briefing on possible contentious news issues. My predecessor, Lizzie Finister was fired for political bias during the previous year's by-election, which was how come I landed the job. After the spot, there was also a fifteen-minute debrief where Eric would applaud or castigate my performance. Fortunately, he was quite diplomatic so I didn't get much of the latter.

With nothing in the news that might spark a flame, I was twiddling my thumbs with twenty minutes to go before I was due on air. I'd already declined Olivia Reitman's offer of tea because she would more than likely turn up with cocoa. I'm not saying the girl was gormless. She was just... well... gormless, really. I'd been working for the station for over a year and she still couldn't get my name right. She called me anything from Clapper to Patter and when I invited her to use my given name, it varied from Justine to Pristine. The one thing Olivia had never called me was Snapper, but there were times when I was on the verge of lending weight to such a soubriquet. To my way of thinking, the only reason she landed and kept her job was because she was Eric's daughter. Not that I disapproved. If she didn't work with and for her father, she'd be unemployed.

With the short briefing over, Eric had other news for me.

"The Christine Capper Interview," he announced, having left his station by the studio to join me near the door. "Early ratings are in and it's official. A huge success."

It was a relief, although I had been told unofficially that it was doing better than okay. "So my future is secure?"

"Worried about your power bills, Chrissy?"

"Aren't we all?" I didn't want to talk about it so I changed the subject. "Who do we have on the short list?"

He hedged. "Very few and I'm not naming any names, but none *of* them can fit us in for a week or two. We could do with slotting someone in this week for broadcast next Sunday afternoon. Do you have anyone in mind?"

"No one. Oh, wait. I tell you what. I'm meeting a potential client tonight. I wonder if she'd be interested in—"

Eric cut me off. "As long as she's not laying accusations. You know the rules, Chrissy. Nothing that might end up in court."

"I'll speak to her."

A little under an hour later, my morning stint done

for another week, I picked up a few bits in the market, and then made my way to Terry's where to my surprise, I found my tea and toasted teacake were fifty pee dearer than last Tuesday.

"I had no choice, Chrissy," he told me. "Do you know how much the rents have gone up in here?"

I recalled the brief debate with Val on Saturday evening. "Dennis and his partners say the same thing about their rent at Haxford Mill."

"It's outrageous." Terry passed me a beaker of tea. "The council say they didn't have any choice."

"Of course they didn't. Someone has to pay for the annual junket to Limoges, don't they?" Limoges was Haxford's twin town. Don't ask me why. I've never been able to fathom it either. Hereford I could have understood. Like Haxford, they have a lot of sheep in Hereford. Well, sheep or bulls or something like that. But Limoges? It didn't even start with the same letter of the alphabet.

I carried Terry's view of things to a table, sat down and tucked in.

Sublime. That was the only word to describe Terry's toasted teacakes. Each and every one was browned to perfection and lavished with butter that dripped into the mouth and onto the tongue.

I had just finished revelling in it when Jill Bleaker turned up. That told me more about the time than anything else. Legend had it that Jill left her desk on the stroke of noon for a one-hour break. I often wondered how she went on if she was in the middle of a phone call at that time. Did she cut it off? "Sorry, but I'm officially on my lunch hour. Call back after one."

That aside, for her to turn up right now meant it was at least ten past twelve and I had overstayed my welcome.

I gulped down my tea with the intention of leaving before she could collar me, but I drank too fast and it went down the wrong way, producing a nasty coughing fit.

"Tsk. Cough like that, Chrissy, you wanna pack the ciggies in, you do."

"I don't (gasp) smoke. Neither does (gasp) anyone else in our house."

Jill was well named. She was a pessimist of the worst kind and there was an in-house joke that went something like, 'things are looking bleaker' and it was usually cracked by someone who had engaged her in conversation. I'd had several chats with her and the jest was one of the many doubling up as a true word.

She did it now. "Sound like a touch of pneumonia, then. Better get to see your doctor for some antibiotics."

It was hard to believe that anyone could come to such a daft conclusion about a simple gagging fit. If I fainted through lack of food (not likely after one of Terry's teacakes) she'd diagnose a heart attack. Even if she didn't suspect a choking session, you'd expect her to suspect a cough or cold. Where did she get pneumonia from?

"Anyway, mind if I join you?"

She didn't wait for my permission, which I couldn't give anyway because I was still gasping for breath, but took a seat at my table.

Those of a generous nature, me included, would

describe her as chubby. Right there and then I was so annoyed that I would have said lardy. Because that's what she was. Worse, she sat down with a mug of tea, into which she poured three sachets of sugar, and on her plate she had a vanilla slice and a chunk of that inviting cream cake Terry had on display. She was only about my age, too. Maybe a year or two older. She talked to me about pneumonia, but she was walking into a coronary. I say 'walking' when what I really mean is waddling.

As a scriptwriter, she wasn't bad. Hardly up to the standards of modern TV (yes, I know that's not saying much) but adequate for a small station like Radio Haxford. As a gossip she was above-average even for Haxford, and you should believe me when I say that our little town held the world record for Chinese whispers. It was coming up to 12:15 and by the top of the hour, the story of my misdiagnosed choking fit would be halfway round the town but by then it would be a case of Jill listening to my death rattle.

She crammed half the vanilla slice into her capacious mouth, chewed on it a couple of times, and then swallowed. I really didn't know how she could get that much food into her mouth at one time, and I had no idea how she managed to swallow it without chewing for at least another five minutes.

She took a moment and mouthful of tea to wash it down, presumably to make room for some air, let it get past the food and into her large lungs, and then she took me by surprise. "A little bird tells me you're joining Georgie Tibbett's mob of no hopers tonight."

I knew exactly what she was talking about, but I

played dumb. "Georgie who?"

"Tibbett. She runs the Haxford Losers Club."

"Oh, right. Yeah. Val Wharrier asked me—"

She ever gave me the chance to finish, but interrupted with serial shakes of the head accompanied by a chorus of tut-tutting which went on so long that it called to mind Skippy the Bush Kangaroo.

"What's wrong with Haxford Losers, Jill?" I asked. It was a way of keeping her engaged on the matter. What I really wanted to know was how she had learned I was going there.

"That depends on how strong your stomach is. Georgie pushes this milk shake stuff. Like Slimfast, but she buys the ingredients and mixes it up herself. She should have named it Yukfast. I've never tasted anything that bad in a long time. If you want to lose weight, Chrissy, talk to your Dennis and get him to bring you some diesel home. Drink that instead. It tastes better and it's not fattening."

I decided she'd led this conversation for long enough. "You've tried a diesel diet, have you?"

"Well, no, but it's common sense, innit? Anyroad up, you'd be better coming with me to Haxford (not so) Heavies. Karen, the lass as what runs it, has the job bang on. One or two biscuits per day as meal replacements and the pounds will roll off."

I cast a meaningful glance over her 'fuller' figure. Not quite full enough judging by the way the last of the vanilla slice disappeared into her cavernous mouth, and to look at her, I guessed the pounds had rolled on, not off.

It was on the tip of my tongue to say, 'Karen

Dawkins hasn't done you much good,' but I didn't. I had more important issues to deal with. Such as… "Who told you I was joining Haxford Losers Club?"

Unfortunately, I asked the question before she had swallowed the bite of vanilla slice, but it didn't stop her answering and I had to look away from the sight of half-masticated icing and custard filling her trap.

"I sold goo. A tittle curd."

After The Incident, Dennis suffered from speech difficulties for a long time. He still did, but I guessed they were deliberate these days. However, after working with Dennis's drivel for so long, Jill's gobbledygook was easy to translate as, 'I told you. A little bird'.

I got to my feet ready to leave, but I was determined to have the last word. "You should tell that little bird to mind its own business or I'll set my cat on it."

Chapter Four

The source of Jill's information troubled me for most of the afternoon, so much so that I managed precious little work on my weekly vlog (yes, despite my modest rise to fame, I was still putting out the vlog and thanks to my radio work, it was more popular than ever).

A three o'clock, with Cappy the Cat nagging to be either fed or let out or both, I abandoned the task, let him out, put down a feed for him, then made myself a cup of coffee and rang Val.

"I told Georgie, obviously," she said when I asked. "If I hadn't she'd treat you as a new member tonight. She's put the word out to the members."

"The word?"

"The word that a local private investigator is joining us to find out what tactics Karen Dawkins is using to filch our members." Val's voice took on a new sense of urgency. "Chrissy what's going on? Why are you asking all these questions?"

"I'll tell you tonight, when we're with Georgie. For now, let me ask, how does she let the members know?"

"Email. Like a newsletter."

"And does it go out only to the members, or does she send it to ex-members?"

"I'm not sure. As far as I'm aware, an email like that, one that's complaining of Karen's underhand tactics, would only go to current members. The more general, canvassing type newsletter goes out to plenty of people who haven't made up their minds."

This all but confirmed my suspicions, but I needed to ask at least one more question. "Do you know Jill Bleaker?"

"Admin-cum-typist-cum general office dogsbody at Radio Haxford? I know of her, and I think we've met a time or two, but it's not like I actually *know* her. Why do you ask?"

I couldn't evade the question any longer. "Because she asked why I was bothering with Haxford Losers Club rather than Haxford (not so) Heavies. The question we have to ask, Val, is how she knew. She wouldn't tell me, you don't know her, so it's practically certain that you didn't tell her—"

"I didn't."

I ignored the interruption. "And I didn't, so who did? The way she talked it was as if she's been a member of Georgie's club at one time and transferred her allegiance to Ms Dawkins."

"Possible. Not while I've been a member, though."

"All right. Let's leave it at that. I'll have a word with Georgie about it tonight. I'll see you at half past seven."

The next problem was Dennis. He answered my call with his typical moans. "What do you want, woman? I'm up to me neck in spanners and a rotten Fiat Punto that won't do as it's told."

"Well, unlike you, I have real problems. Have you

been talking to Jill Bleaker?"

"Bleaker... Bleaker... Gil Bleaker...what kind of motor does he drive?"

"He is a she. She works at Radio Haxford. Large woman. You can't miss her." That at least, was true. For a woman with a shadow like a total eclipse, it would be impossible not see her coming towards you.

"Never heard of her. Is that it? Can I get on now?"

"What about your pals?"

"They've got their own work to do. I don't need 'em helping me."

"No, Dennis. I mean have any of them spoken to Jill Bleaker."

"Well how would I know? You'll have to ring 'em and ask 'em."

"Tell you what, you ask them and ring me back. If I don't hear from you in ten minutes, it'll be a cheese salad for tea and I'll leave it in the fridge for you."

"Hang on, hang on. I do a proper job of work. I need more than rabbit food for me dinner."

"In that case, ask your friends and ring me back."

I cut the call and dropped the phone on the table alongside my laptop.

It was highly unlikely that any of Dennis workmates had had anything to do with Jill. The only one who might have done was Lester Grimes, but he would have met her in the Engine House (known locally as The Sump Hole) and given Lester's predilection for Haxford Best Bitter, I doubted that he would have entertained her. In the unlikely event that he had, they would not have talked about dieting.

In any case, I wasn't sure that Jill frequented the Engine House.

And that left me with a problem and only one possible answer.

Dennis rang long before the ten minutes was up and confirmed that while his workmates had heard of Jill, none of them had ever spoken to her. This was a common situation in Haxford where everyone knew everyone else even if they hadn't actually met or chatted with them. Dennis's information confirmed my sole conclusion. Someone in Haxford Losers Club was feeding information to Karen Dawkins and the Haxford (not so) Heavies. There was a spy in Georgie Tibbett's camp. I was not James Bond 007. I wasn't even Jane Bond 003 and a bit. I hadn't the first clue how to go about unmasking spies.

At half past four, I began the process of getting ready for the evening. You'd never believe how long it takes to put on makeup, mascara, and especially the length of time it takes to get my hair right. Dennis would know what I'm talking about. He moaned about it all the time. And when all that was done, I had to select the right clothing (a pair of loose-fitting pants and a floppy top in a neutral white, large enough to hide the increasing spread of my belly and bottom). It all eats up the minutes, and talking of eating, I had Dennis's meal to cook and stow in the microwave. By the time I was something like ready, it was almost six o'clock.

And throughout this process, I pondered ways and means of uncovering the secret agent determined to sabotage Georgie's operation.

With the time coming up to seven I stood in front

of the wardrobe mirror to ensure I looked the part of a comfortable, cool and confident businesswoman taking a night off to advise a friend of a friend and it occurred to me that I didn't have to expose anyone. I wasn't getting paid for my work, so why should I? All I had to do was give Georgie my thoughts. She could do the rest herself. Unless she chose to hire me to do just that. And with that, the angst came back.

It was all very well for the likes of Sean Connery, Roger Moore, Pierce Brosnan and them. They could usually seduce some drop dead gorgeous girl and get her to spill the beans in bed. My seducing days were where they belonged. Thirty-odd years in the past, and anyway, I was visiting a diet club. Most of the men there (if any) would more likely sport a firkin than a six pack. For those of you who don't know, a firkin is a small barrel with a capacity similar to Lester Grimes on an evening at the Engine House. Not that Lester was fat, but like a firkin, he could hold many pints of beer.

With these thoughts whirling round my head, I scrawled a note for my better half telling him how to deal with his dinner (I mean warm it up, not how to eat it. He was already an expert in that capacity) and left the house just after the turn of the hour. I drove along Bracken Close and waved to Dennis as he was coming in the opposite direction. Typically, he didn't see me. Either that or he was still annoyed and ignoring me. Either way, he didn't wave back.

Up above, the sky was a grumbling collage of cloud with intermittent patches of blue. According to the forecast, the recent poor weather was about to give way to a heatwave. In my opinion, it couldn't come too soon.

At the end of the street, I turned left onto Moor Road, and pulled in outside the Breakfast to Bedtime minimarket where I bought a four-bar Kit-Kat, before continuing my journey towards the town centre, but at the bottom of the hill, where it met the southern town centre bypass, I turned to the right, making for Barnsley Road.

To my way of thinking, the idea of Haxford Health Spa was nothing short of disingenuous. Haxford was listed as one of the unhealthiest towns in Great Britain, and while the basic idea of a health resort was good, the cost of membership was so high that it hardly catered for the town's population, most of who were living next door to flat broke.

Built about four or five years previously – much to the amazement of everyone in the town other than the council who stood to gain a fortune from it – the place stood a mile out of town on Wakey Moor Road, a tributary of Barnsley Road, which led to Wakey Moor, one of the lower stretches of moorland surrounding the town, from where the roads led (in a roundabout way) to Wakefield (known locally as Wakey). A cluster of hi-tech buildings set in open moorland, the spa was all glass, steel, and solar panels, membership would set you back somewhere close on the cost of a year's council tax, and if rumours were to be believed, the price rose with the same, alarming frequency as did the council tax. Beyond that, there were the various classes and treatments to be paid for, and they did not come cheap. It was said that even the cost of a workout in the gym would set you back half a day's wages, and like Sleepy-Byes they employed super-salespeople masquerading as 'health consultants' to sell you membership.

It was rumoured that the food was as you might expect, complex, theoretically nutritious, and priced higher than your common or garden, upmarket restaurant. Fine if you enjoyed seaweed soup and dandelion burgers. Speaking personally I preferred simpler meals like egg and chips (and I didn't know it then, but they did sell them).

Once parked outside the building, I attacked the Kit-Kat with gusto. It was legitimate. I would be spending the evening with a gang of dedicated gluttons, all of whom had to behave like angels so they could pass the weekly weigh-in without attracting too much criticism. I couldn't very well sit amongst them chewing on chocolate, so I needed to gorge on the goodies before I joined them. That's my excuse anyway.

Not only mine. I saw one or two other people on the car park carrying out the same, surreptitious exercise, and I would soon learn that they were Haxford Losers Club members. Indeed, I noticed one woman busily unwrapping what looked like a Cadbury's Dairy Milk, and she had a sticker on her back window, advising others to 'Join the Haxford Losers Club and watch the pounds roll off.' I spotted it when she reversed into a parking spot and I thought, 'Yes, good plan. Get your members advertising'. When I saw the chocolate, I changed my mind. Mrs double-standards needed to be a bit more discreet about feeding her chocaholic tendencies, especially if Georgie Tibbett was as keen-eyed as me.

Val's Ford Focus pulled into the car park at twenty-five past seven, and I climbed out of my ageing Renault (I did a straight swap for it with Haxford Fixers and they got the old Fiat Diablo) to meet her.

"Any further forward?" she asked as she led the way into the hall.

"Not so you'd notice," I replied, and told her of my earlier conclusions.

"You any good with industrial espionage?"

Her phraseology made me laugh. "Industrial espionage? You make it sound like someone's stolen the secret of eternal youth from a medical lab. All I'm saying, Val, is that one of the members may be a plant, working on the quiet for Karen Dawkins."

"I think she already knows that, Chrissy. Any chance you could find out who?"

"Not for free, I couldn't." I gave her my sweetest smile. "Sorry, Val, but as I so often say, I'm not a charity."

She understood and appeared as if she didn't care. "I don't know whether she could pay, but you should take it up with her."

The meeting room was seriously upmarket from Haxford church hall where the last slimming club meeting I attended had been located. In place of old and draughty read warm and air-conditioned. Too warm as it happened. Fortunately, most of the cloud had disappeared, and the evening summer sun shone through the windows which were open to let some real air in. I guessed that in the late autumn, and throughout the winter most of the wannabe slimmers would still be sweating in that room. They'd need to eat more to keep warm before they got there, and the canned air and heat would make them sweat it off.

There were about twenty people already in the room, all queuing to stand on Georgie's bathroom scales and have his/her card marked by the boss woman. Aside from Val, I recognised only one other individual; Tel Wheatley. At one time he played football for Haxford Town FC, a non-league club, and I recalled rumours of him undergoing trials with Huddersfield Town and (dare I say) Sheffield Wednesday. Judging by his shape, the only trial he was likely to get now would be in front of judge and jury for fraud, i.e. describing himself as an athlete. Of Afro-Caribbean descent, he was third or fourth generation British, and I once ran a vlog on Haxford Town, so I knew him to be pure Haxford. The difference between the man in the queue and the man who had graced the turf at Barncroft Stadium, was alarming. He had given up playing about five years previously, and where the team shirt would have flopped and flapped over his flat tummy as he ran around the field, nowadays it was his tummy flopping (and probably flapping) over the waistband of his joggers.

It was easy to see why he had joined Haxford Losers Club, and with but a few exceptions, the same applied to most of the others in line. Without knowing how long each member had been attending, I had no way of judging their progress, but on the surface it seemed to me that most of them weren't winning the fight against fat, and on seeing them I felt comfortable with my weight. I might well be almost a stone heavier than I was before Christmas, but most of these people didn't look as if they'd seen a slim Christmas since they took the Morecambe & Wise show off air. The only way they would be able to run a visual check on certain parts of their – ahem – anatomy would be to stand in front of a mirror.

I had absolutely no idea where that final thought came from. I was not given to such analyses on my own body and I certain didn't check on Dennis's bits, nor any other man, come to that. It just goes to show you how the mind can drift when you've nothing better to do on a summer's evening, doesn't it?

Georgie Tibbett came as a revelation. Slim? When? If you stood her behind a Michelin Man she'd still be easy to see. She was slimmer than Jill Bleaker but only by about one size. Where did she find the sheer neck to establish and run a diet group? I suppose she could be running it on a basis of, 'Do as I say, not as I do,' but it was a bit barefaced.

Val said that Georgie was a few years older than her, but looking at her round face I found it impossible to guess her age. She could have been anywhere from forty-five to sixty. Her skin almost matched Tel Wheatley's – and I bet her appetite did too – but most of her appearance was suntan, whether fake, salon, or Benidorm derived. She was untidily dressed, too, in a blue, sort of three-quarter length top, black, loose-fitting pants which flapped round her ankles, and a pair of black trainers that were caked in what looked like dried mud. They certainly hadn't seen a dash of shoe cleaner in a long time. Her head was topped with a bundle of red hair, and she had a voice to match it: loud. When speaking to one woman, she could clearly be heard all around the hall when she said, "It's not good enough, Heidi. You're supposed to take the weight off, not put it on."

I'd have been tempted to mention kettles and pots and the colour black, but Heidi, a bulky blonde in her late forties, was happy to retort, "It's that slime you make us drink. I don't know what meal it's supposed to replace, but it must be a stray dog's. The damn stuff leaves me feeling hungry."

Her riposte probably explained why I saw her eating a large Dairy Milk in her car.

Georgie was not ready to leave it there. "Like anything that does you good, it's not meant to taste good."

I could think of several arguments against that, not least of which was a few Bacardis. They did me the power of good and they tasted wonderful. The same could be said of McVities Chocolate Digestives, and I'm sure Cappy the Cat would agree with me on that point. He enjoyed lapping up the crumbs.

The weigh-in took a long time, and Georgie handed out only a few congratulations. Most of the time it was criticism that someone had not hit their target weight for the week. Val was one of the few exceptions. She had lost another two pounds. I was impressed. The amount of booze she put away on Saturday night she must have starved herself of food in the three days since.

When everyone was seated (just after eight o'clock) she stood before them ready to go into her weekly lecture, but first she introduced me.

"This lady is Christine Capper. We all know her

from her programmes on Radio Haxford but she's also a private investigator. She's going to look into the manner in which Dawkins seems to know exactly that's going on in this group. Christine is not joining us as a member, although I have to say she looks as if she could do with signing up."

Oh, yes? That remark would cost Georgie Tibbett. I had decided that if she wanted me to take on her case, I would charge her mates' rates: twenty pounds an hour. By opening her trap like that, she had just upped it to my regular rate of forty pounds an hour.

She was still going on. "So be warned, whichever one of you is feeding information to Dawkins and her people, Christine Capper is on the case, and when she unmasks you, you'll have me to face."

She scanned the small audience, obviously looking for signs of guilt, but as she was about to go on, Detective Sergeant Mandy Hiscoe came in. I found this odd. Mandy had lost weight the previous summer when she gave birth to her daughter, Darlene, but she didn't need to shed more. Neither did my son, Simon, and with his appearance behind Mandy, I knew it was an official visit

"Ms Tibbett?" Mandy asked.

"Mrs Tibbett. What can I do for you?"

"Detective Sergeant Hiscoe, Haxford CID, and this is Detective Constable Capper." Mandy gestured at me. "Christine's son. You have to come with us." That last was aimed at Georgie not me.

"What? Whatever for?"

"We need the answers to some questions, luv."

Georgie stood her ground. "But I'm in the middle of an evening's work."

Mandy shook her head. "So are we. Now you either come with us or we arrest you."

Her face flushed with anger, Georgie demanded, "Why?"

"For questioning on the suspicious death of Annie Louise Endicott. Now let's move, Mrs Tibbett."

Chapter Five

Instant pandemonium.

Most of the members were on their feet, protesting they'd paid for the evening's session, Georgie Tibbett was crying foul, but her protests were smothered by the cacophony.

Mandy, ever the professional detective, remained unmoved. She and I were old friends even though she joined the police years after I had left, and I knew her well enough to know that she would not be intimidated.

Because of all the shouts, cries, complaints, no one could make their point, and Mandy was waiting for the furore to die down. I decided I had better things to do with my evening than listen to this rabble of lardies squabbling with the police, so I stood up, moved to the front from where I could look Mandy and Simon in the eye while studying the back of everyone else's head as they faced the two detectives. I looked around for something solid, and couldn't find anything, so I picked up Georgie's hardbound notebook in which she logged everyone's weight on a weekly basis, raised it above my head and with as much strength as I could muster, threw it on the floor where it landed with a loud crack.

It had the desired effect. Silence fell upon the

room and everyone turned to face me.

I beamed a generous smile on them. "Hello, everyone. As Georgie has already told you, I'm Christine Capper, and I'd like you to listen to me for one moment." Satisfied that I had their undivided attention, I went on. "I was a police officer years ago, and I can assure you that it doesn't matter how much you whinge, whine, shout, and scream, Mrs Tibbett will still have to go with Detective Sergeant Hiscoe. In plain English, you're wasting your breath." I focused on Georgie. "Go with them. You don't have a choice, and I know Mandy well enough to know that if you refuse, she will handcuff you and drag you along to the station."

"But I haven't done anything," she pleaded. "I haven't even seen Annie for months."

Mandy took up the point. "In that case, Mrs Tibbett, you have nothing to worry about. Now come with us or we will take you."

"Go with them, Georgie," I advised. "If you need any help, give me a call." I dug into my bag and handed her my business card. "My phone's switched on twenty-four, seven, except when I'm in the studio or recording."

Georgie's anger was reaching an explosive peak. "I have more to do than—"

Mandy tapped Simon's arm, and he spoke up. "Georgette Tibbett, I'm arresting you on suspicion of involvement in the death of Annie Louise Endicott. I must caution you that you do not have to say anything—"

"Wait, wait, wait." This time it was Georgie who cut in on Simon. "This is ridiculous but I don't suppose I have any option."

"None," Mandy assured her.

Georgie turned to her members. "I'm sorry, but we'll have to call it a night." She stared at me. "Consider yourself hired and get me out of this." Her gaze fell upon Val. "Could you issue the shakes and take the money, please?"

"Sure, Georgie," Val replied. "You get it sorted out, and bell me the minute they let you go."

With Mandy ahead of her and Simon behind, Georgie left the hall and once the door closed, the mutter of conversation flooded the room.

Val moved to the front and Georgie's cartons of boxed-up shakes, and I moved alongside her. "Like me to give you a hand?"

"If you don't mind, Chrissy. Each box contains ten shakes, and they're eight pounds a box. They're optional and not everyone uses them. There's also a weekly member's fee. A tenner. So for those who take the shakes, you want eighteen, and for those who don't it's ten."

HOW MUCH? I didn't actually say it, but it was a close run thing. Suppressing my indignation, I commented, "I thought it was the energy companies playing highway robbers."

Val gestured around her. "It's this place, innit? The spa? Georgie tells me they charge her a fortune for hire of the room every week."

"In that case, she should think about renting the parish hall in Haxford." Having delivered my opinion, I concentrated on the members. "Before we start, ladies and gentlemen... gentleman, if any of you know this Annie Louise Endicott, please hang about so I can have a word with you." I focussed again on Val. "Did you know her?"

"Later, Chrissy. When we've got this job done."

"Right. Let's get on with it? Shouldn't take us long to get through this little lot."

Val laughed. "Wanna bet?"

She was right. You wouldn't think twenty people could take so long to deal with. Taking the ten pounds membership fee was the easy bit but when it came to buying the shakes (they all did) most of them couldn't decide whether they wanted strawberry, vanilla, banana, or one of the many other flavours. In addition, when they ordered, we had to find them in the different cartons which, contrary to common sense, were not packed with a single flavour, but sort of haphazardly. Worst for us were the café latte and mocha frappe, and no I'm not turning into a poetic rapper. There were only a few boxes and they were buried under a mass of other flavours. I figured that if she could go to them right away, Georgie Tibbett must have an almost eidetic memory.

We were halfway through the job when Sonny Scott and Irma Orson, two uniforms I knew well, burst in.

"Sorry, Chrissy, ladies and gent, er, ladies and gentleman," Sonny said, "but we've been ordered to impound all those diet packs."

Immediate uproar, but like Mandy and Simon, Sonny and Irma remained unmoved.

"We've already sold about a dozen, Sonny," I complained when the noise settled.

"Not my problem, Chrissy. You'll have to take it up with Mandy. All I know is she's just told us to come and take the lot away." He faced the members. "If you've already paid for some of this stuff, you'd better queue up and get your money back, and while you're at it, make sure we get every box back."

"Just what's going on?" I asked.

"I can't tell you," he replied, "and it's not cos I don't want to, it's cos I don't know. I'm just following orders."

"Isn't that what the guards at Belsen said?" That was Tel Wheatley, still in the queue and speaking for the first time.

"Not very helpful, Mr Wheatley," I said. "I'll speak to Mandy Hisc—"

"Wasting your time, Chrissy," Irma interrupted. "Like Sonny told you, she was the one who gave the order."

"She might not have told you why, but I bet she'll tell me."

It just goes to show how wrong you can be on a warm summer, Tuesday evening. I rang Mandy, I cajoled, begged, pleaded with her but she refused to go into detail.

"Catch up with me tomorrow and I'll clue you up. Right now, I'm acting on information received."

"This is a fine way to treat a friend."

"Not interested, Chrissy."

"Georgie Tibbett just hired me to help."

"I know. I was there. And you can help her. You can let me do my job."

"Arresting her in the middle of an evening's work without taking you to task? Not likely."

"She's not under arrest. She's being taken in for questioning. Cut it, Chrissy, for God's sake. Just let me get on with it and call me tomorrow."

"One thing before you ring off," I asked. "When did this Annie wossnames die?"

"Yesterday. That's as much as I'm telling you. Goodnight, Chrissy." And with that, she cut the connection leaving me to glower at the phone before joining Val for the process of handing back moneys taken.

And it wasn't as smooth and uncomplicated as I make it sound. Everyone we had dealt with before the arrival of the two police officers had bought a carton of shakes, so from that point of view, it was plain sailing, but more than one didn't just want back the cost of the shakes. They also wanted their weekly fee back, and one or two, most notably Mrs Heidi 'Dairy Milk' Flanagan insisted that they would not be back again.

"I'm not paying out good money to a murderer."

"Nobody says she's murdered anyone, Ms Flanagan."

"It's Mrs Flanagan."

"Someone should murder that spiteful cow," called a voice from the back.

"Who? Ms, er Mrs Flanagan?" I asked.

"Who else?" asked the voice.

By now, Heidi had turned to face the woman. "You wanna learn to shut your gob, Keenan."

The woman at the back of the queue, who I now recognised from the membership list as Patricia Keenan, bit back right away. "You're a fine one to talk, Flanagan. The only time your mouth is shut is when it's crammed full of chocolate or some bloke's—"

"Ladies, please—"

"I was gonna say some bloke's tongue," Patricia assured me.

"And she's no lady," Heidi ended her announcement with a scornful laugh. "She's well named, is Keenan. Never seen anyone so keen when she's dropping her knickers for some bloke. Any bloke. She's the only woman in town with 'yours for the right price' written on the front of her pants."

"Yes. I bought them at a jumble sale after you'd done with them."

"Tart."

"Whore."

"Ladies, please—"

"Bitch."

Having run out of derogatory names suitable for mixed company, Patricia left the back of the queue and marched towards Heidi, who prepared to meet her, and for a moment, I thought war was about to break out but before they could come to blows, Tel Wheatley grabbed Patricia's arm and held her back, while Irma Orson stood in Heidi's way.

Order was gradually restored and after talking it over with Val, who insisted it wasn't really our place to say yea or nay, we refunded Heidi and three other people their weekly fee.

I was the unofficial bookkeeper for Haxford Fixers and they were an administrative tangle, mainly because I struggled to read their handwriting. At the side of sorting out Georgie Tibbett's clientele, Dennis and his partners were a dream, and it was getting on for half past eight before we had everything done and dusted, and Sonny and Irma left with the shakes.

I would say we had it all sorted to everyone's satisfaction, but that wouldn't be so much an exaggeration as an out and out lie. No one was satisfied. The grumbling disagreement between Heidi Flanagan and Patricia Keenan rumbled on, only just stopping short of actual violence, the members complained about the high-handed attitude of the police in not only shutting down the meeting but sequestrating the diet shakes, thereby ruining their collective Tuesday evening. All of which gave me the impression that the Haxford Losers Club was as much a social gathering as any inclination to shedding the pounds.

Worse than that, not one of them had a good word to say about Annie Louise Endicott. Miserable, vindictive, nagging, forever spoiling for an argument or a fight. That last comment came from Heidi Flanagan, and considering the way she challenged Patricia Keenan, the words kettle, pot, and black sprang to mind once again.

As we were wrapping it all up and the group began to leave, a tall, gangling man came into the room. He stood about six feet six, and had the kind of bland, lived-in face common to Haxford, but the most striking thing about him was his garb. He was wearing a shell suit in green and black, which probably slotted in nicely with his age – about the same as mine – but it hung on him like a loose sack. I could just make out the shiny toes of black trainers, and half way up his calves both legs had a curious crease across them. He must have been wearing elastic bands at that level to stop the suit getting under his trainers and tripping him up. Odd when you think that a) he was so tall and b) shell suit pants usually had elasticated bottoms. Or maybe his legs were so thin that the elastic wouldn't pinch that close.

"Good evening," he said. "Where is Mrs Tibbett?"

"Unavoidably detained," I replied. "And while we're about it, may I throw the question back and ask who are you?"

"I am Fletcher Leeming." He said it in the kind of voice that really meant, 'I am God and my word is law. You will heed my commandments or suffer eternal damnation.' Overall, it did not fit with his appearance.

Val was sending me frantic signals with her eyes to back off, but after the hassle with Mandy and her team, then the Haxford Losers Club members, I was in too bad a mood.

"I see? And by what right do you come in here asking for her?"

"I am the general manager of this establishment, madam, and I am not accountable to you. Indeed, I would hazard that you need to explain your presence to me."

"Hmm. Got your finger on the pulse eh? Well, Mr Leeming, you manage the place so well that you obviously don't know Mrs Tibbett has been taken away by the police?"

"I...er..."

"Nothing serious, of course. Only the suspicious death of one of her members."

"Oh. I... er... Oh dear."

Val was now playing head tennis, looking at me

with amazement and Leeming with something close on pitying humour.

"What did you want with her, Mr Leeming?" I asked, determined to wring every gram of merciless pleasure out of his discomfort.

"She, er, she owes us for the hire of the hall. I usually call in the middle of her class to collect it."

An odd arrangement if anyone wanted my opinion, but I was too wrapped up taunting him to press it. "Well, that's nothing to do with Mrs Wharrier or me. You'll have to take it up with Georgie Tibbett. If the police let her go, that is. Course, if she's guilty, you might have to wait for your money. Say, fifteen or twenty years."

"I, er, oh, my lord. I'll, er, I'll leave you to finish clearing up. Thank you."

He backed out of the room and Val applauded me. "You met him head on. I don't think I've seen even Georgie do that."

"He got up my nose." I collected Georgie's record book and handed it to Val. "You know, after all that, I think I need a drink."

She grinned. "Me too, and I know the perfect place. Only about half a mile from here."

Chapter Six

Val was right. The Barley Mow stood half a mile from the spa on the road back to Haxford.

When we were younger, Dennis and I would sometimes drive out to the place for a few drinks on a summer's evening. He did the drinking, I did the driving. And the place hadn't changed much since those days. It still boasted a large car park – larger than was necessary considering it relied on passing traffic rather than regular patrons – it still had the traditional and unimaginative horse brasses littering the beams around the bar, and still offered a full range of ales from all over Yorkshire, with a predisposition towards Haxford Brewery's range. The seating had been renovated, and the piped musak was no more, having been replaced by a wall mounted jukebox.

The clientele had changed, too, and I noticed the difference the moment we walked in. Gone were the hikers and ramblers of the moors, and in their place were the sporty types, the fitness fanatics, the poseurs, refugees from the spa, who probably felt that the gym and squash court had cost them enough, and opted for a cheaper post-PT pint at the Barley Mow.

There was worse to come. While Val went to the

bar (she was bigger than me all over and therefore more likely to be noticed and served earlier) I had a good look round the spacious room and clapped eyes on any number of Haxford Losers Club members. Patricia Keenan was leaning on the bar sipping on a clear drink, which I assumed was water but which could just as easily be a large G&T or even Bacardi or vodka. She was chatting to Tel Wheatley who was knocking back a pint of lager like there was no tomorrow while laying an evil eye on a couple further along the bar. I followed his gaze. Of the pair, I didn't know the man, but the woman was Heidi Flanagan. She too was drinking from a tall glass, but the liquid was a pale chocolatey colour with sprinkles and I guessed it might be a Baileys chocolate martini. I couldn't see it being a chocolate milk shake for the simple reason that the bar didn't serve milk shakes. I did, however, notice that now and then her head turned in the direction of Ms (or Mrs) Keenan and Tel, and I could imagine her returning the glower of daggers coming from Mr Wheatley.

Val returned with our drinks, a glass of lemonade for me, a clear spirit for her and a mixer bottle. She must have noticed me looking at her glass because she turned the bottle so I could read the label. "It's all right, Chrissy. It's slimline tonic. It won't affect my diet."

"That depends on what you're mixing it with."

"Gin. What else?" She took a healthy slug. "Ah. That doesn't half hit the spot."

I sipped at my lemonade. "Did you know that the calories in alcohol are known as empty calories?"

Her eyebrows rose. "Really? In that case they

should help with my weight loss."

"No, Val, it doesn't work like that. They're call empty calories because they have no nutritional value and they help you put weight on."

"Oh. Do they? Ah, well, how much am I likely to gain with the odd G&T? Can't be much, can it?" She took another, more cautious sip this time. "You seem to know a lot about it."

"I've been there," I admitted, "and yes, I know that if I don't watch it, I'll be there again sooner or later."

She glanced down at my legs. "Sooner rather than later, Chrissy."

"You know, I really should consider choosing my friends more carefully."

"The Haxford code, girl. Tell it like it is."

"Yes, well, you said you'd tell me about Annie Endicott, but first, how come so many of the Losers Club end up here after the sessions? Or don't they? I mean, is it because the meeting was cut short?"

"No, no. They come here every week. I think it's the way Georgie's running the club just lately. It's all argument after argument."

"I noticed."

"It's not only them. Half the people from the spa come here after they've finished."

"But not Fletcher I'm in charge even if I don't know what's going on, Leeming?"

Val laughed. "Him too, but only now and then. Some of the women call him Fletcher the lecher. He's so tall that for those women wearing a low cut top, he stands close to them and looks down their cleavage when he thinks they won't notice."

"Hmm. I must remember to wear a button-up blouse next time I'm here. If there is a next time." I cast my eye on the bar area again. "What's the story with the Keenan woman and Heidi Flanagan?"

She lowered her voice to a conspiratorial whisper. "Well, don't quote me on this because I got the tale second-hand, but they're both single or divorced or something and like to play the field. It seems Keenan was going out with that man—" She aimed a finger at the man stood with Heidi "— and Flanagan stepped in and persuaded him away. And I'm sure you don't need a diagram as to how Heidi tempted him."

"Knickers fitted with extra-slip grease?"

"That applies to the pair of them, but I think Heidi was quicker on the drawers." She chuckled at the weak witticism. "I don't know that they've actually ever come to blows, but they've been at each other's throats ever since, and this is… what… nearly a year ago."

"A long time to hold a grudge. Especially over a man."

"Exactly. I mean, there's enough of them to go round."

"Precisely. So come on. Annie Louise Endicott."

She was quiet for a moment and I guessed she was working out where to begin. After another sip of the drink, she began, "Bear in mind I've only been with this group for about four or five weeks, so I don't know her that well, but my impression fits with everyone else's. She's about sixty and a nasty piece of work. I actually know her husband better because he does odd bits of winter work on our garden. You know. Tidying it up, getting it ready for the spring."

"And is he as bitter as his wife sounds?"

"A grumbler for sure," Val admitted. "A bit like Tony and Dennis. A bit like most of the working men in Haxford, I suppose. And I have heard him whine about his wife, but I'll bet Dennis and Tony whine about you and me when we can't hear them."

I had to laugh. "Dennis whines about me when I can hear him."

Val obviously did not know the victim well and I tried to think where to go next, but before I could gather my thoughts, Georgie Tibbett walked into the bar. Not only that, but I noticed she'd changed her clothing. In place of the large, flouncy, pale blue top she wore over her black pants, she now sported a smaller, bright red T-shirt, which did nothing to hide her belly, and which only came down to her waist, leaving her behind and large thighs clearly outlined in black, skin-tight joggers.

"Georgie's back," I said. "That was quick. I'm surprised Mandy let her go so soon."

"It's not Georgie," Val said. "It's Karen Dawkins. They're twins."

I'm sure my colour drained. At least, it felt like that. But it could have been something to do with the last time I dealt with twins: the Kalinsky brothers, one good, one not so good.

I challenged Val. "You never said anything."

"Didn't I? Sorry."

"So the dispute between Georgie and Karen could be sisterly aggravation as much as anything?"

"You'd have to ask Karen about that, Chrissy – and Georgie if the police let her go. The way Georgie tells it, the battle is strictly to do with business."

I gulped down most of my lemonade and stood up. "In that case, it's time I had a word with Mrs Dawkins."

"But… But… You can't just walk up to her and lay down the gauntlet."

I gave her a smile flooded with a confidence I wasn't sure I really felt. "I was a copper, remember. In my game you have to strike while the iron's… well, lukewarm at least."

"Well, be careful. She's like Georgie; a snapper, and she might strike you with a flat iron."

It was fair warning, and even though any kind of violence was unlikely to happen, Val's words ensured that I was on my guard as I walked over to tackle her.

Karen was talking to Heidi and the man she had been talking to. He was a stranger to me, and not too well off, if anyone wanted my opinion. He was dressed in joggers and a shabby, loose fitting top, and his mud-stained trainers were just about hanging off his feet. I guessed he was one of Ms or Mrs Dawkins' members, a deduction which stemmed from Heidi's abrupt resignation from the Haxford Losers Club earlier in the evening.

I sidled up to them, and from behind, I announced myself. "Good evening, Mrs Dawkins. I'm Christine Capper."

She turned to look at me, her face a mask of disdain, her eyes blazing, lip curled. "Radio Haxford doing a piece on the Barley Mow, are they?"

"I'm here as a private investigator, and your twin sister has just hired me."

The sour features did not change. "Well, I hope you do better than you're doing already. We're not twins. Georgie is a year older than me."

I gave her a cynical smile. "My apologies. I was working on information received. You've been made aware that Georgie is under arrest?"

"Nothing to do with me."

As far as I was concerned, that was beyond the pale. "She's your sister, for God's sake. Putting aside your efforts to ruin her business, don't you think you should be concerned for her?" Having made the point, I reverted to cool and collected. "Or could it be that you actually shuffled Annie Louise Endicott off her mortal coil in an effort to incriminate your sister?"

Thanks to Val's warning, I expected Karen to throw a punch in my direction, and in the brief second before she struck I tensed my leg muscles, ready to take a half step back.

It never ceases to amaze me how I can get so much wrong. Karen did strike, but not with her fist. Instead, she threw a drink at me. She kept hold of the glass, naturally, but the clear liquid (a strong scent of rum told me it was Bacardi or Pernod probably mixed with soda water or tonic) splashed the front of my white top.

I looked down at the mess, and further down at the ice cubes already melting on the hard-wearing carpet, then glared back at her. "I'll send you the bill for dry cleaning, and I daresay the landlord might bill you for spoiling the carpet."

I took a pace forward, for the first time, I noticed the tiniest hint of worry come into her eyes.

"It's not advisable to mess with me, Mrs Dawkins—"

"It's Ms Dawkins. I'm not married."

"And I don't care. Check me out and you will find that I don't give in. Your sister stands accused of murdering this woman. By tomorrow morning, my good friend Mandy Hiscoe, top dog in Haxford CID, will give me the bottom line, and if I have even the slightest suspicion that you're just simply trying to ruin your sister's reputation as well as her business, then I'll be back and you will talk to me." I switched my focus to Heidi Flanagan. "And the same goes for you."

"Me? What have I done?"

"You were quick to resign from the Haxford Losers Club, and now I find you hobnobbing with Georgie's biggest rival, and it makes me wonder whether you were the one feeding Ms Dawkins the information she needed to steal Georgie's clients."

Leaving them with this dire threat, I turned, and marched away from them.

I hadn't got back to sit with Val, when the man they had been stood with caught up with me. "Mrs Capper."

I gave him the full, Capper glare. "What do you want?"

"A quiet word. If that's possible."

"About?"

"Karen and Georgie. What else?"

I nodded towards a vacant area of the bar, and we made our way over.

"Can I get you a drink?"

I shook my head. "I don't drink with strange

men."

He laughed. "I can assure you, there's nothing strange about me." He offered his hand. "Jonathan Ambrose. I'm a fitness instructor at the spa."

I looked him up and down. Somewhere in his mid- to late-forties, a tousle of fair hair, square shoulders, sinewy wrists, I could well imagine him throwing weights about. A good-looking man in a Haxford-ish way, there was a sparkle of humour which accentuated the crow's feet around his brown eyes, and the slightest hint of a smile played at a slender lips. He wouldn't be my cup of tea, but then, I never look at other men anyway... Well, not very often, and even when I do they're usually film stars and it's nothing more than distant daydreaming.

We shook hands. "A fitness instructor? You don't seem to be making much progress with Karen Dawkins, then. No offence, but she looks more fat than fit. Is that a reflection on her appetite or your work?"

"Can I get you anything?" In response to his question, I shook my head. He signalled the barmaid and ordered a half of lager. "Are you always this confrontational?"

The question was aimed at me, not the barmaid. "No. Not always. But when I come up against people like Dawkins and a loudmouth like Heidi Flanagan, then I'm ready to slug it out toe to toe. And just in case you're wondering, Mr Ambrose, as I said to Karen, I used to be a police officer and now I'm a private eye. These days, as she hinted, I'm a local radio presenter."

The barmaid returned, and after asking again

whether I wanted anything, he paid for his drink, sipped the head off the lager, put the glass down on the bar, and concentrated on me.

"Just to clarify the situation, I'm Karen's partner."

"Business or life?"

"Life, of course, and I don't like to hear her accused of something she hasn't done."

"In that case, the first thing you should do is teach her some manners. My original intention was to inform her that her sister had been arrested, but her attitude precluded that. Make no mistake, Mr Ambrose—"

"Jonathan. Please."

"As you wish. Make no mistake, Jonathan, I won't go away. The last thing Georgie did before the police hauled her away was to hire me to demonstrate her innocence, but my original reason for attending the Haxford Losers Club meeting was to learn who's been feeding Karen information which allowed her to steal Georgie's members."

He took another sip of lager. "You're getting the wrong end of the stick to begin with. No one is feeding Karen any information. They don't need to. That… sludge Georgie offers to her members, the diet shake, is garbage. It's tasteless crap, and from a weight-loss point of view, it's not very effective."

I recalled that during the initial weigh in Georgie was full of criticism for almost everyone. There were only one or two members who had managed to lose any weight. I also remembered that Jill bleaker and Heidi Flanagan complained about the shakes.

Determined not to allow Jonathan Ambrose any leeway, I fought a rearguard based on distraction.

"Looking at Karen, it doesn't appear as if her Haxford (not so) Heavies system is doing much better."

"Granted, but you don't know the history between the two women."

"Is it important?"

"Very. Up until about a year ago, they were very close. Then something happened to bring about Civil War."

"What happened?"

He took yet another sip of lager, smiled at me, and turned a finger to point at himself. "Me."

Chapter Seven

It's a good job I was a professional woman. Otherwise I wouldn't have been able to hide my surprise.

I use the word 'professional' in the sense that I was a private investigator, radio presenter, blogger and vlogger by profession. I say this because the term 'professional woman' is open to all sorts of misinterpretation, especially when talking to a handsome-ish man in a busy pub. That went double on the assumption that he was about to confess some of his dirty little secrets.

Not that I was particularly interested, but of course any information on the two women and their problems might be welcome.

Before he could clarify his meaning, Val came across to me. "I'm sorry, Chrissy, but I have to go. Tony will be getting anxious."

I risked a glance at the clock and read 9:30.

"That's okay, Val. I'll speak to Mandy first thing in the morning, and then catch up with you later."

She left, and Ambrose and I took the vacant table where I sipped on my rapidly warming glass of lemonade, and then asked, "What do you mean their problems arose from you."

He hesitated a moment. "I'd prefer that this was

kept between ourselves."

I shrugged. "As long as it has no bearing on the murder of Annie Endicott, that's fine, but if I or the police uncover any link, then I will be compelled to let them know everything I know. Now please explain what you meant."

He didn't hesitate. "Georgie is divorced, and her marriage fell apart because she had an affair with me. Naturally, this was before Karen and I became partners. At the time Georgie and I met, they were running the diet club together, and as you've already noticed, both were considerably overweight. They came along to my fitness sessions, and to be fair to both of them, they worked really hard. Then as now, we used to meet here for a quick drink after the sessions, Georgie and I hit it off, and then we..."

"I think I get the picture, Jonathan. Please go on."

"Her husband found out, and Georgie ended our affair and put in the effort to save her marriage. Pointless exercise. Within another couple of months, she and her husband split, he cleared off back to Glasgow, Edinburgh, somewhere north of the border, and Georgie came running back to me. Trouble is, by then I was involved with Karen. That started an argument between them, which ended when Georgie punched Karen. End of joint diet club. Georgie went off on her own, started up the Haxford Losers Club and at the time, she was holding two sessions a week in the parish hall. Fletcher Leeming approached her... Have you met him?"

I nodded. "Not only met him but put him in his place. I assume you're going to tell me that Mr Leeming approached Georgie and persuaded her to move the Losers Club to the spa."

"On the button. Worse than that, Leeming arranged for both women to run their sessions on the same evenings; Tuesdays and Thursdays. Things deteriorated when Georgie decided to bring a few members here to the Barley Mow after the sessions. Just to clarify that, Karen has always brought her members here." He gave me a wan smile. "There are those times when it's like war is ready to break out. You might think I'm biased, but I don't believe that Karen is to blame. As far as I'm concerned, it's all Georgie, and she's incensed that Karen now has the kind of settled life Georgie had before her old man went back to Scotland. And if you think about it, Mrs Capper—"

"Christine, please."

"As you wish. If you think about it, Christine, Georgie was in the wrong in the first place when she fell for my – forgive me – theoretical charms."

I wholeheartedly agreed with him, but then, my stand on adultery is well-known. There may be excuses for infidelity, but they're few and far between and rest (as far as I'm concerned) on one of the partners being disabled and incapable. It was a situation I'd been through with Dennis shortly after The Incident, but even then it never occurred to me to stray from the marital bed. True, it did occur to others that I might be getting hard up. Men like Nathan Kalinsky who tried his luck out on the moors during the Stocker affair, and I had to stop him before he could get to no man's land.

Ambrose's admission had left me with an unanswered question, which technically, had absolutely no bearing on the situation, but my inherent nosiness compelled me to ask it anyway.

"You'll have to excuse me, but I can't understand what would prompt a… fit and reasonably good-looking man like you to chase after a couple of women who are – let's be honest about it – overweight. It might sound catty, but I would have thought a man like you could do better."

He chuckled. "With someone like you, perhaps?"

His reply brought a smile to my lips, but I wagged a warning finger at him. "That's not what I meant."

"Pity. Anyway, to answer your question, I feel sorry for today's women. Television advertising, magazines, are all about pressurising women to come up to standards which are often unattainable for your average girl in the street. I say unattainable, but what I really mean is, they can't be achieved without spending a lot of money, and without having the basic requirements in the first place; slim, fit…ish, relatively attractive. You know what I mean." He waited for me to agree before going on. "It seems to me that we're encouraged to judge women purely on their appearance. What about intellect, intelligence, their essential individuality of character? We men are mostly to blame. Ask a man what would be his ideal woman, and most of the choices would come from the pages of beauty magazines and from the catwalk. Speaking as a man, I say we need to forget about the envelope and look at what's inside?"

I was impressed. During the routine course of my busy life I hadn't come across many men with this attitude. Assuming he was telling the truth. And that was slightly questionable considering his fly response to my initial query on his choice of women.

"So the chance of you charming a woman into bed doesn't come into the equation?"

"Initially, no. Obviously, at some stage, we do get down to the, er…"

"Ultra-close and personal?"

"A perfect description, but when I first meet a woman, that's the furthest thing from my mind, and so it was with Georgie, and later on, Karen."

"You never married?"

"Once. It didn't work out, and I'd rather not talk about it if you don't mind."

"None of my business anyway. Coming back to Georgie's problems, let me ask you, did you know Anne Louise Endicott?"

"Annie-Lou? Vaguely, but not well."

But well enough to curtail her full name. I kept the thought to myself and asked, "How likely is it that Georgie poisoned her?"

"Most unlikely. She was a cantankerous woman. Annie-Lou not Georgie. The kind who could start an argument in an empty room, and as I'm sure you've already learned, Georgie is the kind to call a spade a spade and be done with it, but she's not violent and neither was Annie-Lou."

"Georgie's not violent? You said she punched her sister?"

"A love tap, and that was in extreme circumstances."

I chanced another glance at my watch. Getting on for ten, and Dennis would be worrying before long. That assumed my husband actually realised I wasn't there, but if one of his favourite car chase films was on TV, there were no guarantees of such.

"It's time I was getting home. Thanks for your help, Jonathan. I'm sure Karen will keep you updated on progress once I get Georgie out of police hands."

Still slightly suspicious of him and his claim to be a 'new man', I watched for him following me from the bar to the car park, but he didn't.

Heidi Flanagan did though.

I didn't realise it at first because I was looking across the car park, seeking my trusty Renault, when I noticed Fletcher Leeming sat behind the wheel of a largish saloon, a Vauxhall or Toyota or something. I don't know, do I? Motor cars are Dennis's thing, not mine. His head was bowed and he appeared to be faffing about with something. Leeming I mean, not Dennis.

It was no business of mine and I didn't think I had anything to say to him right now, but Heidi announcing her presence put him out of my mind.

"Fancy your chances with our Mr Ambrose, do you?" Her voice brimmed with challenge.

"Not particularly," I replied, "but if I did, is it any of your business?"

"No, but you has to watch him. First time I went out with him, he had me laid under him five minutes after we came out of the pub."

"Yes, well, I don't do that kind of thing."

"Oh. So your pants are welded into place, are they?"

"Do me a favour, Mrs Flanagan. Go home before I take exception to you."

She sniffed. "Only trying to warn you."

"I don't need your warnings, thank you."

I climbed into my car and Heidi headed back to the pub, only to be intercepted by Leeming when he got out of his car and joined her at the door. I recalled Val's warning about him and as he met Heidi, he slipped an arm around her shoulder and looked down. Well, he had to really. He was head and shoulders taller than her. I couldn't remember whether she was wearing a V-neck top but she didn't appear to object and when they disappeared into the pub, they were all smiles…. Like old friends.

Heidi was not the prettiest woman I'd ever come across. Come to that, she'd need to make an effort to achieve 'plain', which meant that there were two ways of looking at her experience of Ambrose and her approach to Leeming. On the one hand, it lent a degree of credence to Ambrose's insistence of looking beyond the mere physical when he first got involved with a woman, and it also said that Leeming was not particularly choosy. On the other hand, if the tale I'd heard of conflict between her and Patricia Keenan was true, perhaps she was one of those women ever ready to leap on a man and if Ambrose had her 'under him' as quickly as she said, it didn't entirely put him on the New Man pedestal.

I climbed into the car, started the engine and pulled out of the car park onto the road home.

Away to my right, to the northwest, the midsummer evening was a gorgeous, pearly twilight, almost as light and bright as the day, and it reminded me of younger years, the days before Dennis and I became parents, evenings when we would stay out deliberately late, visiting outlying pubs like the Barley Mow to put off the thought of work in the morning which hung over us like some nightmarish demon. I was sure life was simpler then. At least we didn't seem to bump into harridans like Heidi or lotharios (if Mrs Flanagan had it right) like Jonathan Ambrose, and these days, it seemed that Dennis worked ever-longer hours to ensure our income, and when I had a case on the go, it tended to haunt me until it was resolved.

And so it was now with Heidi's supposed warning to me. I couldn't make up my mind whether it firmed up my opinion of her as 'easy' or highlighted Ambrose's 'let's treat women better than we ever have' plea as flannel. Or possibly both. Flannel, flattery, call it what you will, was something he'd inadvertently suggested when I said he could do better than Georgie or Karen. His reply, 'with someone like you, perhaps', came across as a shallow means of testing the waters. Was it a joke, or did it signal the real Jonathan Ambrose?

All this was based on Heidi telling it like it really was. She'd had a glass of… something, and her verbal exchange with Patricia Keenan told me that she was of the same confrontational mould as Annie Louise Endicott (according to legend). It would be unwise to take Heidi's word for anything, much as it would be silly to accept Ambrose's insistence on his approach to women.

Beyond that, did it really have anything to do with Mrs Endicott's suspicious death? Superficially, the answer was no, but Ambrose did refer to her as Annie-Lou. To me, that was a sure sign that he was more familiar with her that he was ready to admit.

Focussing on the death of Annie Endicott, I

realised that right there and then, I knew next to nothing. No one had a good word to say about the poor woman, but that did not mean anyone in the Haxford Losers Club or the Haxford Health Spa had any involvement in her death, and I couldn't see how Ambrose might be hooked into it. Unless Mrs E was young-ish and he'd tried his luck with her, but Val's description of Mr Endicott didn't really support that. If it was so, there must have been a sizeable age gap between the pair. Then I recalled the Leach case. Petra Leach was a good few years younger than her husband, but that had to do with large amounts of money and I doubted that your average gardener/handyman would be in the same league.

I was halfway up the hill to Bracken Close when Dennis rang and took everything out of my mind. I was on hands free so I made the connection.

"Where are you?" he asked. "I were expecting you home an hour ago."

"Things got complicated. I'm about five minutes away so I'll tell you when I get in. Be a love and put the kettle on. I'm gasping for a brew."

In Haxford at the height of summer it never got properly dark. Even in the early hours of the morning if you looked to the north you could still see the distinct glow of twilight. As such, it was light enough for me to reverse into the drive when I got home. It was something I didn't normally do for fear of hitting one of the gateposts, but my confidence had been soaring for some months now and that sure-footedness extended to my driving skills.

I found Dennis in the kitchen, brooding over a mug of tea.

"What a shocking evening," I announced. "Everything all right with you, love?"

"Is it heck as like. That's why I was wondering where you'd got to. Uncle Billy's dead."

He'd already prepared a beaker of tea for me, and I was about to tell him of my evening, but I scotched that, sat opposite him, took a welcome glug of tea, reached across the table and held his hand. "I'm so sorry to hear that, Dennis." I frowned. "I didn't know you had an Uncle Billy."

"He were t' black sheep of the family. I've never even met him, so you don't have to be sorry. It's what's been happening since he snuffed it that's bothering me." He fixed my eye with a determined stare. "Somebody's been in touch with me mam, and I think it's a scam. You're the private detective, I reckon you could find out."

"Oh."

This was unprecedented. Dennis acknowledging that I was a private eye – something he'd always disapproved of – and in need of my services. Normally, the only thing he needed me for was cooking his meals, and that was because when it came to cookery he was positively lethal. I've said many times that he could only manage toast because the toaster was fitted with a timer. Whenever he tried his hand at anything else, the result was invariably overcooked, often to the point of bursting into flames as the wallpaper behind our cooker could testify.

"Tell me what you know," I invited.

"According to what they told Mam, Billy died about two months ago, but he died interstate. I think they mean on an interstate, which is some kind of motorway in America. What he was doing over there, I don't know."

"The word is intestate, Dennis. It means he died without leaving a will."

"Oh. Does it? Anyway, because me dad's dead, Mam is Billy's only living relative, and whatever he's left behind is hers. Trouble is, Chrissy, they want all the details off me mam. They want to see her birth certificate, wedding certificate, proof of where she lives, and all the rest of it, and I reckon somewhere down the line, they'll be asking for her bank details and password. But Mam's not daft. She rang me and told me what was going on, and I said I'd have a word with you, see what you think."

I took another sip of tea. Family complications I could live without right now, but on the other hand, I'd always got on fairly well with Eunice Capper, and I didn't like the idea of her falling victim to scammers.

On the other hand...

"It's possible, Dennis, that they could be legit. They're called heir hunters. They look out for intestate deaths, and then chase up the families. When they're successful, they take 10 percent or more of whatever's left after it's all been sorted out."

His face brightened. "Oh. Right. So Mam could be in for a bob or two?"

"It's possible but let's not count any chickens. Tell you what, I have some business to attend to at the police station first thing in the morning, and when I'm done with Mandy, I'll nip along and see Eunice. Get all the details from her and I'll look into this company. How's that?"

He smiled. "And what will you want in return? A bit of attention tonight?"

I laughed. It was not often that Dennis dropped such hints. Not these days anyway. I let him down gently. "That's not a bad idea, but I'm sorry, I'm far too tired. Maybe tomorrow night."

Chapter Eight

An early call from Mandy saw me parked outside Haxford police station at 9:15 the following morning.

The promised heatwave had arrived. A cloudless sky, temperature already rising, just the faintest trace of sweat breaking on my brow, were all signs that the last thing I needed was a confrontation with Sergeant Vic Hillman, known to all and sundry (courtesy of me when I was a police officer) as Minx.

"What do you want, Capper?"

I gave him my sweetest smile. "I want to know where you learned your skills in ignorance and arrogance, Minx."

"Call me Minx again and I'll—"

"Minx."

A brief silence followed and I was the one to speak first.

"There. I've called you it again, Minx. What are you gonna do about it?"

"Just clear off, Capper."

"I'm here to see Mandy Hiscoe."

"She's busy, now do like I say and get lost."

"She's expecting me, you idiot. Now get on the horn and tell her I'm here."

A minute or two later, having received

confirmation from Mandy that she was waiting to see me, he let me pass and I made my way into the station.

The aggravation between Vic Hillman and me went back to my days as a police officer when he decided he didn't like me. Dennis told me that Hillman, the motor company, had two popular models, the Imp and the Minx. At six feet something there was nothing remotely impish about Hillman, so I christened him Minx, and the nickname stood. Not that anyone other than me and a few of Haxford's hard case lags dare utter it to his face, and I only found the wherewithal after I ceased to be Constable Capper.

Mandy was a different proposition to the senior officers in the Haxford station. She was (technically) head of CID, but that was because she refused to take the inspector's exam. She did not want to leave Haxford, and promotion to the rank of inspector would compel such a move. She came under the command of Paddy Quinn, another Haxforder who had made the move to Huddersfield when he was promoted. I often said you could hear the cheers on the day he left town. Mandy and I were good friends, Paddy and I, good antagonists.

Mandy and Paddy were like chalk and cheese. Whereas he was confrontational, Mandy employed a listening ear, where he would accuse, Mandy would hold back until she was sure of her ground, and so it was that fine, sunny morning.

"We released Tibbett under interrogation at about ten o'clock last night," she explained. "We're waiting for toxicology reports, and I could hardly hold her for another forty-eight hours while we get them."

"When Sonny and Irma took away all of Georgie's stock, I guessed that you suspected poisoning through the diet shakes, but I can't understand what led you in that direction. If Paddy was in charge, I'd say it was a shot in the dark, but I know you better than that, Mandy."

"Her husband. Walton Endicott. He likes to be called Walt, and you can't blame him. God knows where his mother and father got that name from, unless his old man had done time in Walton nick." Mandy allowed herself a sly smile at the last idea. "He told us she was fine first thing in the morning when he left for work. She rang him later, told him she didn't feel well. This was an hour after she'd mixed and drunk Tibbett's diet shake. At least he says that's what she told him. He got home at four in the afternoon and she was dead, and he rang us. Obviously, we're waiting for the post-mortem and toxicology results, but according to the pathologist, it does look like poisoning." She shifted the subject sideways. "What's the score between you and Georgie Tibbett? You looking to shed a few pounds?"

The suggestion did not endear me to her. "What is it with everyone? Do I look as if I've put on weight?"

Mandy laughed. "Would you like me to tell you the truth, or would you prefer me to lie?"

"For your information, I've put on a few pounds, but not that much. It's not as if I'm a tub of lard, is it?"

"No, Chrissy. Course you're not."

That last comment came out in an 'anything for a quiet life' tone but I had a busy day ahead of me so I let it go and proceeded to give her the bottom line on Val's request at the weekend, which led to my attendance at the Haxford Losers Club meeting the previous night.

"But if you were listening, Mandy as you led her away, she hired me to prove her innocent. And I have to say, if it was the diet shake which poisoned the Endicott woman, it's unlikely to be Georgie's doing. I mean, she doesn't make them herself, does she?"

"That's the whole point, Chrissy. She does. She has a sort of mixing-cum-packaging set up in her garage. She buys the ingredients, blends them, and then packs them in boxes of ten. Sells them for about eight quid a box."

"I already know the price. I had to give those people their money back last night." I buried the memory. "It must take some hours, making these up."

"Keeps her busy most of the week, so she says. She also says that it's a legitimate operation. She has visits from the relevant authorities, Foods Standard Agency, Trading Standards, she has a food hygiene certificate, and according to her, she's scrupulously careful to ensure that nothing other than the necessary ingredients and flavourings gets into those cartons. If that's so, and it turns out that Annie Louise Endicott really was poisoned by the shake, then it has to be deliberate."

"No one else has access to the place?"

"According to her, no. She's divorced apparently, lives on her own."

"I knew she was divorced. Did she tell you anything about the aggravation between her and her sister, Karen Dawkins?"

"She mentioned it, yes, but as far as I'm concerned, it's not relevant. At least, not right now it isn't."

"What about the motive for killing Mrs Endicott?"

"Again, she says she doesn't have one but according to our information, she and Endicott didn't get on."

"Yes, and according to my information, Annie Louise Endicott didn't get on with anyone."

"Now there, I would have to agree," Mandy said. "The few people we have spoken to, her husband, her neighbours, tell us that she was a total dragon. The kind of woman who'd pick an argument if you just said good morning to her. Tibbett admitted that she got a lot of grief from the moment Endicott joined her diet group, but she denies that it would lead to murder. I'm sorry, Chrissy, but as things stand, without evidence of the contrary, I don't believe her." Mandy closed the case folder, leaned back in her chair, and asked, "Can you throw any light on the matter?"

I shook my head. "Not right now. I spoke to a few people last night in the Barley Mow, and they agree that Georgie is an unlikely killer. A snapper, yes, outspoken, yes, but not a killer."

"Well, you know the script. If you come across anything which might help push us one way or the other, let me know. Failing that, once we get the post-mortem and toxicology results, we'll move ahead, and if that points to Georgie Tibbett's guilt, then I'll have no choice. I'll charge her."

"I'll keep you posted." I got to my feet, and then had second thoughts. I sat down again. "Tell me, do you know anything about a man named Jonathan Ambrose?"

"Mr, I'm a fitness fanatic? An instructor at the Health Spa?"

"The very man."

"From a personal point of view, I know a bit, but from a police point of view, we've nothing on him. Why are you asking?"

"I had a lengthy chat with him last night concerning the aggravation between Georgie and her sister, but somehow or another it became a discussion on his affair with Georgie, and his current relationship with Karen. He also tried to hit on me in a roundabout way."

She laughed again. "Has anyone ever told you that you're the original Mrs Iron Drawers?"

"I'm a one man woman," I insisted, "and I'm not going to apologise for that."

"Well yes, he does have a bit of a rep, Chrissy, but when you talk to him he tries to come across as an innocent man but one for whom the ladies simply fall at his feet… Or other parts in that general direction. He's not exactly my flavour of the month – any month – so I can't tell you any more than that."

"It's enough. It confirms my suspicions of him."

"You don't think he's involved in this business, do you?"

"No. Not really. But you never know. He pretended not to know Annie, but then let slip with her more casual name, Annie-Lou. It's enough to make me suspicious." I stood up again. "Right. Time I was on my way. I have to call on my mother-in-law."

"Eunice? How is she?"

"Pushing eighty, but sprightly as ever. I'll give her your regards."

I came out of the police station to bright, even hotter sunshine, climbed into the car and promptly opened the windows on either side (thank heaven for electric windows) and the sunroof.

The sheltered housing estate where Eunice lived was one of the better quarters of Batley Road Estate. When Dennis's father died, we felt obliged to offer her accommodation at our place, but she turned us down. She preferred to be with her elderly friends in the small development where they were well looked after. Not that the place was a residential care home. Every flat was self-contained, and they had a resident warden on twenty-four-hour call, and she had a couple of assistants who worked various shifts to ensure that there was weekend and holiday coverage.

I rang her before I left home, told her I was coming to visit, and asked if she wanted anything from the shops while I was on my way over, but she said no. The warden and her assistants did all her shopping for her. All the same, I stopped off at her local Breakfast to Bedtime minimarket and picked up a small box of fancy cakes before driving round to Jutland Mount.

She must have seen me get out of the car because before I could press the entry call (a standard installation for those who were semi-ambulant) to let her know I had arrived, she pressed the release button and let me in.

Eunice Capper would reach her eightieth birthday just before Christmas. Between us (that's Dennis and me, his sisters, brothers and their spouses) we had planned a huge celebration for her, but she'd already warned us off.

"Just send me the money. I'll celebrate with my pals here."

As mothers-in-law go, she was the best sort. She never interfered, was always ready to listen, and when it came to disputes between her eldest son and me, she did not take sides. Whether she was like that with Dennis's brothers and sisters, I don't know, and didn't really care. Dennis's father, Malcolm, spent all his working life as a plumber, employed by Haxford Borough Council. As a consequence, he had an excellent pension when he retired. Like many women in Haxford, Eunice spent her working life in a woollen mill, the result of this was when Malcolm died, she was left comfortable income-wise. The upshot of all this was Eunice never put upon us. Despite her age and notwithstanding the vagaries of mild arthritis, she remained fiercely independent as her refusal to live with us after Malcolm's death demonstrated.

"After speaking to our Dennis yesterday, I'd a feeling you'd turn up, Chrissy," she said as she made her slow way to the kitchen and switched on the kettle.

I followed her into the kitchen, reached into a cupboard and with a familiarity born of the many times we'd visited, took down two beakers. "This kind of thing is my stock in trade, Eunice. I couldn't live with myself if I didn't check this out for you."

"So you think it's iffy, do you?"

"I'm not saying that. It could be quite legitimate, but better safe than sorry."

She gave an aged chuckle. "If they're picking on a silly old sod like me, they must be getting hard up."

Showing off even more familiarity, I dug out teabags then ferreted about my bag for my sweeteners. "You don't know how much damage they can do just by stealing your identity."

There was a brief hiatus while she made the tea, and I instructed her to go back to the front room while I brought the cups through.

Eventually, settled in front of the dormant fire, I led into the discussion. "How long is it since you've seen Billy?"

She brought the beaker to her lips with shaking hands, took a sip, and put it down on a little occasional table alongside her armchair. "A long time."

"I told Dennis I didn't even know he had an Uncle Bill."

"He was a bad 'un. There were only him and Dennis's dad, you know. My Mally was a grafter. Straight from leaving school he got his apprenticeship with the council and aside from his holidays and the times when he was sick, he never took a day off. Billy went the other way. He were… Let me think about this. Two years younger than Mally and he was forever in trouble with the police. After he left school he got a job. It didn't last long, and I can't remember who he was working for, but he turned to thievery, robbing, burglary, and he'd served his first stretch before he was eighteen. Six months for breaking into the Co-op on Halifax Street. He wasn't out a year before he was inside again, this time for longer, and after that, the family disowned him. Anyway, he moved to Leeds or Bradford. Somewhere in that area, and the last we heard he was living with some lass on an estate somewhere near the motorway. That's as much as I can tell you. If this business is upfront, Chrissy, I don't know what Billy's left behind, but it won't be much."

I disagreed. "You never know, Eunice. Maybe he had a house, and if the mortgage has been paid off, it'll have value. Once these heir hunters get it sold off, whatever's left is yours."

She laughed again and shook her head. "You don't know him. There is no way any bank or building society would have given him a mortgage. He was an out and out crook."

I wasn't disposed to argue. "We'll have to see. How old would he be?"

She lapsed into thought for a moment. "Well, let's see. I'm eighty in December, Mally would be eighty-one in April, and that means Billy must be seventy-eight or seventy-nine. I mean, I'm not surprised he's clocked out. I'm just surprised they say he's got something to leave behind which is what makes me suspicious."

"Have you got the letter you received?"

"It weren't a letter. They rang me."

"Oh. Dennis just said they'd been in touch, and I assumed that they'd written to you."

"Nowt of the kind." She reached across and

picked up her mobile phone, a surprisingly modern smartphone. "Here y'are. T'number should be in there somewhere."

I accessed the call record, found the number, checked with her that it was the correct one, made a note of it and passed her phone back.

"All right, Eunice. I'll get off and leave you in peace, and when I get home this afternoon, I'll get a trace on this number, find out who they are, and I'll let Dennis know. Failing that, I'll pop in and see you again when I'm in the area."

"Good girl. I always said our Dennis picked the best when he married you."

Chapter Nine

It was a little after eleven o'clock when I left Eunice, climbed into my car, and rang Val. After bringing her up to speed on the previous evening's information, I asked for Georgie Tibbett's address.

"East side, Chrissy. Hold on. Let me give you her number."

There was a pause before she came back online and dictated the number to me. I read it back to ensure I had it right, she agreed, and then added a warning.

"Word is that she's steaming, so tread carefully."

I forced a laugh. "Haven't you realised yet, Val? I don't tread with kid gloves."

"Okay. But don't say I didn't warn you."

I broke the connection, and made the call to Georgie. As Val predicted, she was in a foul mood.

"What the hell do you want?"

"I need to speak to you, Georgie. If I'm to have any chance of clearing your name, I need a lot of information from you."

"Since when does it have anything to do with you?"

"Since you hired me last night."

"Well, in that case, consider yourself fired."

What had I said to Val about refusing to be

intimidated? Her attitude almost made me back out there and then, but I held my ground. "It doesn't work like that. You hired me. Right away you owe me for two hours work. That's sixty pounds to you. I'll take cash. Can I come round and collect it now?"

"That's outrageous. I didn't take you on. I was—"

"You did. In front of witnesses. Your precise words were, quote, consider yourself hired and get me out of this, end quote. As far as I'm concerned, and in law, that is a contract. Now, are you going to pay me or would you like me to make a bigger effort to get you out of this mess?"

After a short pause, she let loose with a stream of invective using several choice words I'm sure I'd never heard before from a woman. Or maybe that's a sign of my old-fashioned attitude, a sign of times past when women generally did not curse and swear like that.

When it was over, she gave me her address, off Barnsley Road, not far from the Barley Mow and the Health Spa.

"I'll be there in fifteen minutes," I told her, "and as I said, I'm quite happy to take cash."

I cut the call without giving her the opportunity to complain further. If she had any more to say, she could say it when we were face to face.

The place wasn't difficult to find. Built in the 1980s, it was a small development of several streets, mostly semi-detached houses with the occasional detached place thrown in for good measure. Georgie lived at 12 Newgate Crescent, one of the semi-detached places, with a huge garage at the top of the short drive. That would be her mix and pack factory, I decided as I climbed out of the car.

I walked up to the front door, rang the bell, and turned away to study the finely mown lawn and pretty little hedges at the roadside. Having met her only briefly the previous evening, she didn't come across as particularly garden-proud, but if she was making anything like serious money from her diet group, it wouldn't be too much of a stretch for her to hire someone to deal with it.

The door opened, I turned and smiled, and she glowered back. When she spoke, her voice was the hiss of a deadly snake. "I'm not gonna start a slanging match on the doorstep. You'd better come in." Leaving the door open, she turned and marched into the house.

What did I say about her not being garden-proud? She wasn't particularly houseproud either. Her furnishings had a good few years on their back, and the general aura of neglect was made worse by bits and pieces strewn here and there: cushions, items of clothing, magazines, even the TV remote. A mahogany display cabinet stood against one wall, and even at a quick glance, the dust was enough to make me run for home, grab a tin of Mr Sheen and come back to give it a quick once over.

She flopped into an armchair while I stood leaning over the three-seater settee. "How much did you say? Sixty, was it?"

Why was I such a soft touch for people like her? She had done nothing but rant almost from the moment I met her, first at her members, then the police, and now me over the phone. She deserved nothing. No pity, no sympathy, no quarter, and yet I felt sorry for her. She stood accused of murder, her business hovered on the precipice of complete collapse, and even if she wouldn't admit it, she needed help not more grief from me.

She was fishing about in her purse when I moved round the settee, and sat half facing her. "Put your purse away, Georgie, and instead of screaming at the world, try listening to me."

She closed the purse, but the anger was still there. "What? What do you want?"

"To help. I know Mandy Hiscoe, and in one respect you're very lucky. If it had been Inspector Paddy Quinn, he'd have remanded you at the station until they had the post-mortem and toxicology results. Mandy has a job to do, but she's fair. She'll listen. All right, she still thinks it's you, but she listened to me this morning, and if I can turn anything up to prove your innocence, or at least cast doubt on your guilt, she will take notice."

"It wasn't me." The anger had gone now, faded as quickly as it had materialised, and it was replaced by pleading.

"And I believe you. I spoke to your sister in the Barley Mow last night, and also spoke to Jonathan Ambrose. He told me all about your history, but no matter what antagonism there might be between you, he doesn't believe you're a murderer, and neither do I. But if I'm going to help you, you need to give me a shedload of information."

Her shoulders slumped, and I detected the first hint of total defeat in her. When she looked up, her eyes were begging yet again. "I don't think I can afford you."

"Let's not worry about that for the moment. There are other ways you might be able to pay me." I realised there were any number of interpretations on that statement, not all of them salubrious, and I hurried on to clarify my meaning. "You could, for example, allow me to interview you for Radio Haxford – but only when this business is cleared up. Alternatively you could sponsor my vlog. It only costs fifty pounds, and that would run for a month. And I wouldn't pressure you for immediate payment."

She pulled in a deep and shuddery breath. "This just about leaves me at rock bottom. I didn't think things could get any worse. Divorced – my fault – the guy I was seeing – Ambrose – shacked up with my sister, and now the cops are looking for me for a crime I didn't commit."

I knew she was going to be hard work. "Let me make you a cup of tea, and then we'll talk."

I left her sitting there, made my way into the kitchen, and switched the kettle on. Scouting through the cupboards for a couple of cups, I noticed the same lack of basic housekeeping as I'd noticed in the front room. The cups I found were stained brown, hinting that they'd never been properly cleaned after use. The black hob was covered in grease, desperately in need of a non-scratch cleaner, and when I checked in the fridge for milk, I noticed the same stains I'd seen in Hazel McQuarrie's before I and the residents of Bracken Close set about cleaning up her house.

Eventually, I carried the cups back to the living room, and sat with her once again. I took a sip of tea.

"There. That's better."

For any private investigator there is a call for occasional disingenuity – is there such a word? What I mean is, it's incumbent upon us to tell the occasional fib. In this case it wasn't so much a fib as an outright lie. Even though I'd made the tea with my advanced housewifely skills, it tasted awful. Cheap teabags, milk perhaps on the turn, and cups that hadn't been properly cleaned since they came out of the factory.

Now, however, was not the time to get into arguments about Georgie's housekeeping. Beneath the anger, there was a lot of pain, a lot of self-pity, and she needed encouragement not criticism.

"If I'm to help, Georgie, I need as much information as you can give me on Annie Louise Endicott, your dealings with her, and on your manufacturing process, plus any other information you think might help."

She shrugged and drank some tea. "What can I say? I didn't like the woman. Hell, I can be argumentative, but she left me at the starting gate. She only ever turned up two or three times, and she did nothing but carp and gripe."

"Did you not think of throwing her out or something?"

"I couldn't afford to. I can't afford to lose any members. Why do you think I get so het up about Karen pinching my people?" She fumed for a moment, obviously trying to bring her thought process under control. "Let me tell you how it is. You obviously know that Karen is my sister, and we used to run a diet group between us. We had a good beat on things, but at that stage, money wasn't too important. I was married, Brian was a lorry driver. He was away from home quite a lot, but he earned top-class money, so whatever money I brought in was just jam and cream on top of the bread-and-butter. Then Karen and I signed up for Ambrose's fitness classes. Within a month, he sweet-talked me into his bed. It went on for a few months, someone opened their mouth to Brian, there was a head-to-head, I ended the affair and I promised Brian I'd put matters right. He brooded on it for a while, then decided he couldn't forgive me, and called it a draw, packed his bags, cleared off back to Kilmarnock. He didn't take anything from the house, and he didn't want the place. That was fine. I had somewhere to live. But I was also lumbered with a large mortgage." She was close to tears when she looked into my eyes. "Right now, Mrs Capper, I'm behind with that mortgage. It won't be long before the bank applies for repossession. The only money I have is the trickle that comes in from the Haxford Losers Club. Now that I've been accused of killing Endicott, even that's gone. I don't know where I go from here. Down, I suppose. I'm not quite at rock bottom but it's only one more step. I didn't kill her but be honest, I'd probably be as well off in prison. At least I'd get three meals a day, a roof over my head, and a bed to sleep in."

Listening to the sorry tale, my first thought was that she had paid an appalling price for a lack of judgement i.e. jumping Jonathan Ambrose. Never mind 'paid', she was still paying, and it was easy to understand why she might find a life sentence appealing. As she said, her basic needs would be taken care of. But there were other angles, not least of which was justice. It was wrong for her to go to prison for a crime she did not commit, and listening to her, I knew she was innocent.

How to encourage her?

"I can see how bad things are, Georgie, but you will never climb up again while you're in prison, especially serving a sentence for the crime you had nothing to do with. Let's go back to basics. After the business between you, Karen, and Ambrose, you set up the Losers Club in the parish hall."

"Karen moved her group to the spa when Ambrose persuaded her. I got going in the parish hall, and a couple of months later, Leeming asked me to move to the spa on the same evenings as Karen. He said the competition would be good for both of us. The room rental is extortionate compared to what I was paying, but I did it. All right, I wanted to give Karen a slap in the face, but it never worked out, and like I said, I've hit rock bottom."

"Okay, so how did Anne Endicott come to join your group? I mean, did she pick you up on your advertising, or was it word-of-mouth, or what?"

"Her husband, Walton. Odd name. Prefers to be called Walt. He's a self-employed gardener and handyman." She gestured vaguely through the front windows. "You might have noticed that my lawn and hedges are quite tidy. That's Walt, not me. He calls once a fortnight, tidies bits and pieces up. Doesn't charge much. Twenty pounds, something like that. And he also works at the spa."

"And he must have mentioned your diet club to

his wife."

"He told me he would, and a week or two later, Annie turned up. She didn't really need to lose any weight. She just had a bit of a pudding in the middle. A bit like you."

I suppressed my irritation but I swore that if one more person mentioned my weight, it wouldn't be Georgie Tibbett looking at a life sentence. It would be me.

She was still talking. "From the word go, she was nag, nag, nag. When she turned up at the second session, she was complaining that the shake was tasteless crap. To be honest, I'd agree with her, and I mix it myself. It has to be like that because I need to keep costs down, so I cut back on the flavourings. Getting back to Annie, I should have booted her out, but like I said, I couldn't afford to." She turned the pleading on once again. "But I didn't kill her. How could I? If I'd poisoned even one of the shakes, it could have gone to anyone... Well, anyone who asked for the particular flavour she bought."

"May I ask what flavour that was?"

"Mango. Worst of the lot in my opinion, but then, that fitted with Annie's sour attitude."

I considered my options for a moment, and in order to distract her, I said, "Tell you what, why don't you give me one of the shakes and let me try it for myself?" I smiled. "I promise I won't slate you online."

She disappeared into the kitchen and I heard her pass through into the garage. She returned a moment later and handed a single shake to me.

"It's strawberry, but you might not taste too much

of the flavour."

"Thanks. I'll give it a try." I dropped the sachet into my bag. "I accept everything you say so far, Georgie, and right now I don't know any more than you. The police suspect poisoning, but that will come out at the post mortem. Are you absolutely certain no toxic chemicals could have got into your manufacturing process?"

"Impossible. I have a degree in food science and technology from Leeds University. I know what I'm doing. I'm ultra-careful about mixing the powders, and I have the backing of the Foods Standards Agency and I have a five-star hygiene rating from the local authority. There is nothing in those powders other than nutritional ingredients, and it's always been that way. When I worked with Karen, we did special, meal replacement biscuits for the members. We baked them here, in my garage and I've never had any problems… until now."

"In that case, we have to ask who else would want to poison her and point the finger at you. Karen?"

She shook her head. "Definitely not. We're sisters. All right so we don't get on too well, but that's down to Ambrose. Talk about fast. I ended our affair, and three days later, he was practically living with Karen. A month after that, he really was living with her. I was well pigged off, but she wouldn't poison one of my members just to pay me back for slapping her across the face."

"And what about Ambrose himself?"

"Again, the answer is no. I think he knew Annie – don't ask me how – but why would he want to poison her? You said you've spoken to him. You must have guessed what he's like. With him, it's anyone in a skirt and how quickly can he get their knickers off."

I smiled. "That's not how he describes himself."

"Yes, well, he's quite skilled with the bullplop. He's a charmer, and like an idiot, I fell for his charms. There's no one to blame but me, Mrs Capper."

"Christine, please."

"Whatever. I can't see why he would want to get rid of Annie Endicott."

"Then what about her husband?"

She chuckled, but it was an empty, humourless laugh. "Walt moans and groans almost as much as Annie did, but they'd been married a long time. If he wanted to get rid of her, I'm sure he would have done it a long time ago."

"There are two other people I need to ask you about," I said. "Heidi Flanagan and Patricia Keenan. Neither of them had a good word to say about Mrs Endicott."

"You'd be hard pressed to find anyone who did, and it's true that Heidi and Patricia can be vicious so-and-so's, but I can't see any reason why they would go to the trouble of poisoning Annie. They can do enough damage with their mouths."

I drank the rest of the disgusting tea, and got to my feet. "Leave it with me I'll need to talk to all of these people individually, and I'll see what I can turn up. Mandy has promised she'll let me know when she gets the post-mortem and toxicology results, and we'll take it from there. If I can make a suggestion, it's that you need to lighten up. There's an old saying. When you're down, the only way you can go is up."

Chapter Ten

I checked the time the moment I got back into my car. Quarter past twelve.

Accessing the web on my smartphone, I checked up on the phone number Eunice had given me, and it belonged to a company called Foulsham, but they weren't located in that Norfolk village. Instead they were in South London, and when I looked up their website, they were an accredited property and probate company. I logged the number on the mobile's directory. I would need to call them later to check that the call Eunice had received was from them, but at least I could tell Dennis something.

Clearing the screen, I rang him. "Where are you, Dennis?" I asked when he answered.

"At work. Where do you think I am?"

"I know you're at work, but Haxford Mill is a big place. Are you actually in the workshop?"

"For now, yes. But I'm on my way to the Snacky in a few minutes to get me dinner."

"Good. I was going to suggest meeting you there. I'll be there in about twenty minutes, so when you go up to Sandra's place, order me a salad sandwich and tea, and I'll catch you there."

"And I suppose I'm paying, am I?"

"You're a gentleman, Dennis, and the gentleman

never allows a lady to pay."

"Gentleman? Last night you were calling me a mental gen… or summat like that."

"Just do it and I'll see you in twenty minutes."

In fact, my reason for going to the mill had little to do with bringing my husband up to speed on Foulsham heir hunters, more to do with Walton Endicott. A self-employed gardener, he had to be mobile, and if Dennis and his pals hadn't serviced the man's car at some point, at least one of them was sure to know him.

Haxford Fixers rented a double unit on the ground floor of the mill, close to the wall which ran along the riverside, but Sandra's Snacky, just about the most popular place in the mill, was on the third floor. The number of comments and hints I'd taken concerning my weight, it was logical for me to climb the stairs. If nothing else, it might burn off a few ounces. Logical, yes, desirable? Not on a hot day like this. When I got there, I took the service lift up to the third floor, and as I emerged into the Snacky, Dennis and Greg Vetch, the latest partner to join Haxford Fixers, were settling down to their meal which looked and smelled like steak pie, chips and peas.

"I've paid for your butty," Dennis told me, "but you'll have to collect it yourself." Having announced that, he got stuck into the pie and chips.

I hadn't seen Sandra Limpkin for a couple of months. The last time I called at the mill, she was holidaying in Benidorm with the Haxford Over 50s Club. Not that she actually qualified as over fifty. According to my information, she had a couple of months to go yet before she passed her half-century but she had never allowed trivia like that to stand in the way of enjoying life.

A smashing woman, if a little blunt and noisy, I'd known her for a good number of years and she was always pleased to see me.

"Looking thin, Chrissy," she greeted me. "Salad sandwich, wasn't it?" She looked at my tummy. "What you need is a solid diet of stew and dumplings followed by sticky toffee pudding twice a day. Get some weight on you."

"Everyone else is telling me I need to lose it."

She laughed and patted her belly. "It's great having a bit extra oomph on you at our time of life. Men prefer meaty women."

Grateful as I was for her comments, I elected to be as fly as her. "I'll be sure to let Dennis know."

She cackled as only she could. "Oh. Like that, is it? Well, tell you what, if Dennis isn't coming up to snuff, let me introduce you to one or two blokes who'd do a proper job for you."

"I'll pass, thanks, Sandra." She handed me my sandwich and tea, and I prepared to walk away, when a thought occurred to me. "Tell me, do you know a man named Jonathan Ambrose?"

"Johnny boy? Yes I've had the pleasure... Well, let's say, he had the pleasure. All I got was a backache. He's not as good as he thinks he is. I'm telling you, Chrissy, if you're looking for a bit on the—"

I cut her off before she could state the obvious. "I'm not. But I am on a case, and his name has cropped up."

"Well let me tell you, he's only interested in two

things. Horizontal PT where and when he can get it, and emptying your purse because he's always broke."

I smiled. "Thanks, Sandra."

This was news of a kind that Jonathan Ambrose would not (for obvious reasons) want general nosy parkers like me knowing.

I left the counter, zigzagged my way through the various tables, and sat alongside Dennis, facing Greg.

"Did you chase up those people for Mam?" Dennis asked as he finished off his meal.

"I got the number from Eunice and I ran a web check on them. They are upfront and official, but I've yet to ring them."

My other half frowned. "Well, if they're official, why do you need to ring 'em?"

Across the table, Greg chuckled. "Just because you've got a call from their number, Cappy, it doesn't mean to say it was them ringing you."

Dennis was still puzzled, but I thanked Greg for his perspicacity. "Most people don't stop to think about it," I said, "but you're perfectly correct. I'll ring them later this afternoon, when I get home, and just make sure that they really are pursuing probate for Billy Capper's estate."

"And what if they're not?" Dennis asked.

"Then the next time they ring, Eunice needs to tell them where to go."

My husband was looking more perplexed by the minute. "I can't work out what's happening here."

"Forget about it, Dennis, and concentrate on the engine in whatever piece of old junk you're working on." I bit off a piece of my sandwich, chewed, swallowed, and washed it down with a wet of tea. "Have either of you come across a man called Walton Endicott?"

They both laughed. "Old Wally?" Greg asked. "Hates being called Wally. Prefers Walt. Him and his missus live on Sheffield Road Estate. He's a miserable old bugger, and his wife's even worse than him. Talk about a battleaxe. If she'd been on our side when the Vikings invaded, they'd have legged it back to Denmark or Sweden or wherever they came from."

Dennis took up the tale. "He used to bring his van for servicing, but we haven't seen him for a coupla years now. Last I heard he was servicing it himself, and prepping it for MOT."

Chewing on another bite of sandwich, I puzzled over my husband's last remarks. "He's a mechanic? I was told he's a gardener."

Greg shook his head. "And he is, but he does his own mechanicking. I think he used to work for the council but he went solo when they put the parks and gardens work out to contractors."

"That squares with what I've already been told," I said. "Anyway, his wife is dead. She was poisoned a couple of days ago… or at least, that's the theory according to Mandy Hiscoe. What price it was Walter?"

Dennis disagreed immediately. "Won't have been him. They were well matched as a pair. Grousers, both of them. Innat right, Herriot?"

Herriot was Greg's nickname, based on nothing more than his surname, Vetch, which sounded like vet. It was a little thin in my opinion. Dennis had always been known as Cappy, but that was logical enough considering his surname, Capper. In Greg's case, they had originally called him Good Boy on the basis that his surname sounded like 'fetch' and when you throw a stick for a dog and it brings it back, you pat the dog on the head and say, 'good boy'. Greg wasn't too keen on that so he became Herriot.

He confirmed Dennis's opinion. "The pair of 'em could moan and groan for England, but I don't think there's anything vicious about either of them, and if Annie's been poisoned, you might think that Wally is in prime position, being a gardener at all, but it's not likely."

I finished the last of my sandwich. "All right. What about a man named Jonathan Ambrose?"

"You keep away from him," Dennis said. "He's bad news for any woman. If he comes on to you, let me know. I'll sort him out."

Now I laughed. "What are you going to do, Dennis, hit him over the head with your spare tyre?" I looked down at his slightly distended waist. and laughed again. "I met him last night in the Barley Mow, and frankly, he'd make mincemeat of you."

"That's not what I meant when I said I'll sort him out." He looked to Greg. "Do we still service his car?"

"If we do, I haven't seen him."

"Well, if he's after you, Chrissy, you tell me, and I'll make sure his wheels come off while he's trying to get his arms all over you on the back seat of his car."

The slight on my fidelity irritated me but before I

could say anything, Greg put his two pennorth in.

"You sound as if you don't trust your missus, Cappy. If I'd had a wife like Chrissy, happen I'd still be wed to her."

Dennis went on the defensive. "I do trust her. It's Ambrose I don't trust."

"Your support is touching, Dennis," I said. "Last question."

"Make it quick. We're due back downstairs so Grimy and Geronimo can get their dinner."

"I'll be as quick as I can, love. Three women. Karen Dawkins, Patricia Keenan, and Heidi Flanagan."

Once again, it was Greg who got in first. "If I hadn't met Patricia Keenan, I'd still be married."

I frowned my disapproval. "I'm sorry, Greg. I mean, I know nothing about you and your ex-wife, but I've always believed there's no excuse for adultery."

"I'm not complaining. It was my fault because I should have kept away from Keenan. I knew what she was like. A piranha. She can strip a man to the bone in seconds. According to the tales I've heard, Heidi Flanagan's the same. As for Karen Dawkins... Never heard of her."

Dennis, too, shook his head. "Me neither. Sorry, lass, but you're on your own." He got ready to leave. "You won't forget to check on that company who rang Mam, will you?"

"The minute I get home, Dennis. I'll catch you both later."

"Aye. At three o'clock," Dennis said.

I frowned. "Three o'clock?"

"Snoddy's coming to suss out the kitchen, isn't he? I told you I wouldn't leave you alone with him. I'll be there for three."

I'd forgotten and really I should have thanked Dennis for reminding me, but his lack of trust in my judgement forbade any such gratitude.

They left but with a check on the time, I decided I was in no hurry. I'd had their views on the Endicotts, Ambrose, and the three women, but I thought it would be useful to get those of their business partners, Tony 'Geronimo' Wharrier and Lester 'Grimy' Grimes, especially Lester. In the same way that Dennis came under my influence, so Tony yielded to Val's steely eye and determination. Lester, like Greg, was divorced, twice in Lester's case, and he put himself out and about Haxford more than any of the other three. If anyone was possessed of a more in-depth knowledge of Patricia and Heidi, it would be Lester.

I was disappointed when Tony was the only one to show his face.

"Hello, Christine. Dennis and Greg said they'd just been talking to you."

"What happened to Lester?"

"He said he had to go to town for spares. We all know what that means."

I giggled. "I didn't know the Engine House sold electrical spares."

Tony smiled and made his way to the counter.

Lester's love of Haxford Best Bitter was legendary, and his favourite bar was the Engine House where he could indulge his palate and knock out a few numbers on the karaoke on those evenings when it was on.

Tony joined me a few minutes later, but in contrast to Dennis and Greg, rather than a full meal, he'd settled for a sandwich and a beaker of tea.

"Val will feed me when I get home and I don't have Dennis's appetite," he explained.

"I've heard of horses that don't have Dennis's appetite," I quipped. Many a true word, and so on, there was more than an element of truth about that. I'd never met anyone who could eat like Dennis, and what was more annoying, he never put on so much as an ounce in weight.

"Did you particularly want to speak to Lester, Christine?" Tony was always more polite and erudite than Dennis.

"Both of you, as it happens. I've already spoken to my other half and Greg, and I'd like to know what you know. First, the Endicotts, Anne and Walton."

"I know Wally. Not well, but I do know him. Val brings him in to do the garden now and again and we used to service his van. I'm sorry, but I don't know his wife at all. Val did tell me that the poor woman died a little while ago, and the police are suspicious."

I nodded, and gave him a brief outline of the previous night's events and my inquiries this morning.

"All I can tell you, is the same as Dennis and Greg. I wouldn't have thought Wally was capable of murder, but then again, I really don't know him that well."

"What about Jonathan Ambrose?"

"I know of him, but I've never actually met him."

"Karen Dawkins, Patricia Keenan, and Heidi

Flanagan?"

Once again, Tony shook his head. "Sorry, but I can't tell you anything. I don't know these women."

I got to my feet. "Okay, Tony. I'm sorry to spoil your lunch."

Another smile. "It's quite all right, Christine. It makes a change to have some kind of intelligent conversation here."

From there, I visited the counter once again, and picked up a couple of cream cakes before leaving the mill and climbing into my car. It was time for a planning session; a euphemism for going home and indulging my appetite, and for once I knew that Cappy the Cat would be the most faithful feline this side of Frodsham. I don't know why I said Frodsham. It was just that I needed another word, preferably a location, which began with the letter F.

Why did I know? Because he would spot the cream cakes.

Chapter Eleven

The reality was that Cappy the Cat greeted me with his usual scorn. I think he was actually pleased to see me, but he preferred not to let me know. He certainly wasn't slow to hit the food bowl when I put it down for him, and once he had wolfed that down, he wrapped himself round my legs a couple of times indicating that it was time to open the back door and let him out so he could terrorise the bird population of our back garden and pay his customary visit to the Timmins's lawn where he would leave his calling card.

For myself, I was tired, and tempted to drag the sun lounger out onto the decking where I could grab an hour's sleep in the afternoon sunshine. But I couldn't. As always, I had more on my mind, bits and pieces which needed attention, not least of which was ringing Foulsham Probate & Property Services and hanging around for the visit of the hitherto legendary Barry Snodgrass. Beyond that, I also needed to track down Patricia Keenan, Heidi Flanagan, and Walton Endicott. That last might be a little touchy. It was early days to be questioning him about his wife's activities and her demise, but I would need to talk to him.

British to the core, a cup of tea was first on the

list, complemented by one of Sandra Limpkin's delicious cream cakes.

It never ceased to amaze me just how keen my cat's olfactory senses were. Carrying my tea and the cake out onto the decking, I had barely settled down at the garden table when he came back over the fence from the Timmins's yard and joined me. Normally, he would walk straight past and ignore me, but as I predicted, the little tyke knew perfectly well that I had a cake and that he would get the crumbs and some of the cream. Less than a quarter of an hour later, he was staring at me, rasping in my direction, as if asking whether there was any more. I ignored him, and he eventually floated off indoors, to re-emerge again after another minute, and station himself on the corner of the decking close to the wheelchair ramp we'd had installed after The Incident. That sentry point was Cappy the Cat's favourite. It allowed him a full view of the garden from where he could keep an eye on the hooligan sparrows and starlings and the thugs of the local pigeon and magpie population.

Cake consumed, tea drunk, my appetite temporarily satisfied, I could feel waves of fatigue sweeping over me, my eyelids began to droop and I yielded to the inclination. It had been a hectic morning and early afternoon, and if I could just snatch a quick power nap, I'd be ready for the fray.

An hour later, with the clock telling me it was quarter to three, the chirping of my mobile, woke me. I checked the menu screen. My mother-in-law. I made the connection. "Hello, Eunice. Is there something wrong?"

"No. Well, I'm not sure. I just thought I'd better tell you that they've rung again. These foulmouthed people."

"Foulsham Probate and Property, you mean?"

"Whatever they call themselves. They're pestering the backside off me for my birth certificate, wedding certificate and stuff."

"I looked them up, Eunice, and they are legitimate. I meant to ring them, but I got tied down on a case. I'll give them a ring now, just to make sure that it really is them chasing you. I'll call you back in about fifteen minutes."

Killing the connection, I called up the company's number and hit the connect button.

"Good afternoon, Foulsham Probate and Property. Selina speaking."

I put on my poshest radio voice. "Good afternoon. I'm ringing on behalf of my mother-in-law, Mrs Eunice Capper. She's received at least two telephone calls from your number. I'm just checking up to ensure that the calls were from you and not someone cloning your number."

"I'm sorry, but I can't discuss individual cases. If you get Mrs Capper—"

I cut her off. "I appreciate that but this is a frail, seventy-nine-year-old lady, and she's understandably anxious having received unsolicited calls – supposedly from you – concerning the recent death of her brother-in-law, William Capper, and she's frightened that you may be trying to steal her bank details."

With regard to Eunice, the word 'frail' was stretching a point. She was tougher than a dustbin full of old boots.

Selina sounded suitably outraged. "We are an honest, law-abiding company. We go to considerable time and expense tracing potential heirs, and when we contact them, we do not take advantage of them."

"And considering we're two hundred and something miles away from you and none of us has ever heard of you, how are we supposed to know that?"

"I—"

I decided I'd heard enough of her standard script, and interrupted again. "Will you please listen to me? I realise you're in South London, I appreciate that anyone who lives north of Hackney is alien to you, but we tend to speak plain English up here in the frozen north. I repeat, I'm not interested in Billy Capper's estate. I'm not interested in your company's bona fides. I'm simply trying to establish that you people contacted my mother-in-law. That's all. Now please put me through to someone who's dealing with this matter. Once they can confirm that they've been in touch with my mother-in-law, then I'll go away and leave you in peace to polish your nails."

She asked, "The lady's name again?"

"Eunice Capper, Apartment 3, Jutland Mount, Haxford, West Yorkshire."

"Hold the line a moment."

Hold the line a moment? It sounded more like an order than a request. The woman didn't even say please.

She went away and the sound of Frank Sinatra singing *Fly Me to the Moon* came on. I hated it. The song, I mean. Mind, I couldn't stand Sinatra either.

He'd barely got past spring on Jupiter and Mars when there was a click and Selina came back online. "I've spoken to Lindsey, the person dealing with this case, and she confirmed—"

"I'm sorry, but I'd prefer to speak to this Lindsey personally. Now please put me through."

Sinatra came back on the line again and a short while later, another connection was made.

"Good afternoon, Mrs Capper. I'm Lindsey Sandals. How can I help you?"

With a name like Sandals I'd bet that she took some stick at school. "Okay. My name is Christine Capper, I'm a private investigator and local radio presenter in Haxford, West Yorkshire. I'm married to Dennis Capper, and it's his mother, Eunice, who's been receiving telephone calls purportedly from you. I'm simply trying to establish that it is you and not some scammer trying to steal her identity and/or her savings."

"I see. And how can we confirm that you are who you say you are?"

"You can ring Eunice when we're through."

"Very well. I'll do that. For the record, we are trying to get in touch with Mrs Capper regarding the estate of Mr William Capper. As far as we can ascertain, she is his only living relative and that only by marriage. We need some form of identification and confirmation of her address before we can proceed."

"Right. I'll ring Eunice right away, but before I do that, could I ask that in future, you speak to me, not Eunice."

"As and when Mrs Capper authorises it."

"I'll make sure she understands that."

"Very good. And you are?"

I was tempted to ask whether she had forgotten her hearing aids but I cooled my ire. "I am Christine Capper. I'm married to Eunice's son, Dennis, and that's twice I've had to tell you. I appreciate you're being careful, but it would help if you actually paid a little more attention."

And with that, I ended the call before she could protest further.

I took a few deep breaths to settle my irritation then rang Eunice and asked her to make the necessary arrangements.

With that out of the way (almost) and my annoyance cooling off, I turned my attention to the case against Georgie Tibbett.

Georgie would tell me where I could find her sister, and with luck, Greg would put me onto Patricia Keenan. The difficult one would be Heidi Flanagan. As far as I was aware, only Jonathan Ambrose knew her personally – and I do mean personally – and after everything I'd heard about him, I didn't really want to speak to him again unless it proved absolutely necessary.

Tracking down Mr Endicott would not be too difficult. At a pinch, Mandy would tell me where I could find him, and I was about to ring her when it occurred to me that he was a self-employed gardener. He and his phone number should be easy to find on the web.

I was right. Inside a couple of minutes, I had his website and phone number, and I was about to call him, when Foulsham's rang me back.

"Christine Capper," I announced.

"Is that Mrs Capper?"

I recognised Lindsey Sandals's voice and almost asked if she still had not found her hearing aids. "Yes, it's Christine Capper. Did you speak to Eunice?"

"I have, and she's authorised you to speak on her behalf. Do you have time to speak right now?"

"Yes."

"Very well. As I explained earlier, we are a probate and property service, and at the moment we're dealing with the estate of Mr William Capper. Technically, he was your uncle."

"Not mine. My husband's. As I understand he died intestate."

"He did."

"And I don't suppose you're willing to say what the estate amounts to?"

"No. Not at this juncture. We don't know the position regarding creditors and other outstanding disbursements, and, of course, we don't yet know that the Eunice Capper we're seeking is your mother-in-law. She needs to understand that this can be a time-consuming process. It can take anything from a few months to over a year."

From the kitchen I heard the door open then close and the mutter of voices. Dennis and Snodgrass, I guessed. I needed to get Mrs Footwear off the phone.

"Especially if there's a property to be sold." I smiled to myself. "I told you. I'm a private investigator, and I used to be a police officer. I have a better than average understanding of the law. I have one final question for you, Mrs Sandals. How much will your services cost Eunice?"

"Nothing." She hastened on to clarify her answer. "That is to say, nothing up front. When the estate is settled and we have a final amount, we will deduct fifteen percent for our services, and the remainder will be credited to Mrs Capper's bank account."

"And if Eunice should predecease that situation?"

"Then it will be disbursed according to her will."

"Fine. I think that's all."

"Good. I have to say, Mrs Capper, I don't think I've ever come across a potential client or a relative of such as abrupt and rude as you."

"You started it... well, your telephone operator did. And if you think I've been rough with you, you should see me when I'm working on a case or interviewing local politicians on the radio. Anything else?"

"No. We'll be in touch with Mrs Eunice Capper once we have confirmation of her identity."

"And I'll get copies of those documents to you as soon as I can. Can I send them as email attachments?"

"Of course. Could you give me your email address? Just so I know it's from you and not someone masquerading as you."

Clever, I thought. It's where the argument started.

I read out to her, she read it back to make sure she had it right, and I killed the call before ringing Eunice again. I told her what had transpired and asked her to get the necessary documents ready. "I'll pop in tomorrow and get them scanned so I can upload them through my email," I assured her.

With that out of the way and the clock now reading a few minutes past three, I dropped everything, and scurried through to the kitchen where I found Dennis and Barry Snodgrass sat at the table drinking tea.

Chapter Twelve

It wasn't really a surprise that he was about our age, mid-fifties. He had a mop of crinkly, greying hair, and a ruddy complexion, which had little or nothing to do with sunburn. Massive hands were closed around a beaker of tea, and I noticed that the skin was red and wrinkled, as if he worked in water for too long. Many people would consider his skin colour to be indicative of high blood pressure, but I was smarter. I didn't know what it meant, but it really had little to do with blood pressure.

"This is our lass, Snoddy," Dennis announced. "Chrissy, this is Snoddy."

We shook hands and his massive paw, buried mine.

"I believe your proper name is Barry Snodgrass."

"That's right, Christine. But everybody calls me Snoddy." He frowned. "Everybody but Grimy, that is. That idiot calls me Snoggy."

"Well, Barry, you can call me Chrissy. All our friends call me Chrissy, don't they, Dennis?"

"They do."

"The one exception is Dennis, who calls me 'our lass'." I took a seat alongside my husband. "Has Dennis told you what we want?"

"According to him it's just a bit of painting."

I gave Dennis my most meaningful stare. The one that said, 'I wish you'd mind your own business'.

Switching my attention back to Barry, I suggested, "Let me show you exactly what I want." I stood up, and invited him to join me over by the cooker.

Dennis had built and installed the kitchen many years previously, and by rights, we really should have ripped it out, and replaced the entire arrangement, but when we asked for quotes, they came in at anything up to £10,000, and for once it wasn't just Dennis tightening the purse strings. I refused to spend so much on what I considered a moderate refurbishment.

The wall was tiled both above and behind the cooker, but that line of tiles only extended for about eight or nine inches above the level of the hob. Above that was wallpaper, a sort of pinkish design with cups and saucers, jugs, tubs of flour, sugar, and so on. When we first papered the kitchen, it looked wonderful. Nowadays, thanks to one or two incidents with Dennis and the chip pan, the lower levels, i.e. those just above the cooker, were scorched. At the time, the tiles didn't come out of it too well either, but with a bit of healthy scrubbing, I managed to get those back to something approaching their original, brilliant white. The wallpaper was (theoretically) washable, but the only way I would have got the scorch marks off was to use an abrasive, like a Brillo pad, and I could only shudder at the thought of what that would have done.

The worktops were all a shade of granite, with a fleck pattern, and on them were the customary appliances and containers needed by most households: bread bin (Brabantia, if you please) toaster, kettle, and microwave.

Above the level of the cooker, either side of it, was a range of cupboards where I stored cups, plates, drinking glasses, and a range of foodstuffs, like biscuits, cereals, etc. They ended flush to the wall by the back window, which these days looked out on the conservatory. The cupboard doors couldn't be touched, but the carcases needed a fresh coat of paint.

We had some halogen lights at ceiling level above the cupboards, but the main lighting in the kitchen was a double strip in the centre. Beyond all that of course, we had under the counter fridge and freezer, dishwasher and washing machine, and another couple of cupboards in which I kept the routine detritus of any household: cleaning materials, dishcloths, and so on. There was even a set of leg and knee support bandages which Dennis had needed after The Incident. On the other side, just inside the side door to our bungalow, was the pantry – Dennis's name for the place where we stored tinned foods, my ironing board, and laundry bags.

I took Barry on a tour of the kitchen, telling him exactly what I wanted. The carcases of the cupboards painting, fresh tiling behind the cooker, fresh wallpaper in those areas where it was needed, and that was not just above the cooker and tiles. There were other areas, albeit narrow strips between and just above cupboards where we had papered, and there was a small wall between the side, exit door, and the conservatory door which would need fresh covering. The ceiling was in need of a coat of paint.

Throughout all this, I could see Dennis from the corner of my eye, and I swear he was turning white at the thought of spending a fortune.

Eventually, we came back to the table, and Barry sat with a notebook, tallying up the potential cost.

"Tell me, Christine, the tiled area behind the cooker. Have you ever considered taking the tiles up to ceiling level?"

"No. Because if we did, I know which idiot would have to get the stepladders out of the garage, and climb up to clean them. I'll tell you what, though, it wouldn't be a bad idea if you could pull the cooker out, and re-tile from the skirting board upwards, but add another, say layer or two of tiles above the current level." I dropped another sour eye on Dennis. "At least that way, when he tries to cook chips again, we may be able to clean up properly."

Barry pursed his lips, shook his head. "To be honest, you could do with an extractor hood."

At this point, Dennis, glad of the opportunity to express his irritation, interrupted. "No chance. The cooker's too far from an outside wall. You can't run it past the window, because that just leads into the conservatory. Anyway, we have an extractor fan by the door." He gestured behind him at the side door, which led out to the narrow path between the house and the garage.

"We just don't use it that often," I said. "One of us is too panicky about the cost of electricity."

Barry shrugged. "All right. Do you want to get your wallpaper, or do you want me to bring a book of swatches?"

"I'll choose it. If you can just tell me how many

rolls."

"Four," he said with absolute conviction. "Ceiling colour?"

"White," Dennis said.

"Ignore him, Barry. I want something a little warmer. What about a nice shade of magnolia?"

He nodded. "I can do that for you." He scribbled away again, then ran his pen down the line of figures, obviously totting up. At length, he pencilled in the total, turned the notepad to face us, and said, "That's your total. It includes materials and labour, but obviously, if you're buying the wallpaper yourself, that's not included."

When I saw the figure – slightly over £400 – I found it satisfactory, but I thought Dennis would have a heart attack.

"I don't know, Snoddy. I'm not saying you're ripping us off but—"

"That price is absolutely perfect, Barry. The only question now is, when can you start, and how long will it take?"

"Chrissy—"

"Shut up, Dennis. Barry?"

He looked around the kitchen again. "All up, two days, maybe three. I tend to be on the job early, half past eight, and I usually stick at it until half four."

"I'm not sure whether Dennis has told you, but I work as a private eye, and there are times when I have to go out. I can't avoid it. You'll be okay left on your own with Cappy the Cat, won't you."

"Cappy the Cat? Isn't that what everyone calls your old fella."

"Yes, I know, but when we got the cat, Dennis

wanted to call him Cappy, but I thought that would get confusing. I don't want Dennis coming along for a worming tablet, do I? Now, Barry, when can you start?"

"I can spend tomorrow getting the materials together, after that, it's only a case of waiting for the wallpaper from you, and we're in business. How's about the day after tomorrow?"

"I think we need to talk about this," Dennis said.

"You're right, Dennis," I agreed. "We do need to talk about it. But Barry, the day after tomorrow is great. I'll make sure I'm here first thing in the morning."

After a little fussing, during which I could see Dennis becoming more and more agitated, Barry left us, and while Dennis saw him out of the house, I made fresh tea, preparing for my other half's assault when he came back in.

He didn't let me down.

"What the bejeebers are you playing at? Four hundred nicker for a lick of paint, and a bit of tiling?"

"You forgot the bit of papering, Dennis."

"I could have done it for—"

"When can you do it, Dennis? You work anything up to fifty or sometimes sixty hours a week and whenever I want anything doing in this house, it takes a back seat. Crikey, it's taken us six months to get this far with Barry Snodgrass. If I wait for you, I won't get it done this side of Christmas… next year. The price is reasonable, he can get on with the job, and I'm happy to pay for it. Am I making myself clear?"

"And you're paying, are you? Cos I'll tell you

this, Snoddy won't take plastic. He'll want cash."

"I'll pop into the bank the next time I'm in town, and make sure I've got the cash for him. Now is that it? Are you going back to work or not? Because I have other business I need to attend to."

He finished his tea, got to his feet and glared. "I took two hours off this afternoon for you."

"No you didn't. You took if off because you thought I couldn't handle the negotiations and it's not done you one ha'pporth of good."

"Whatever. I'll have to make that time up. I'll see you at seven." And with that, he stormed out of the house.

With Dennis gone, I moved back to the conservatory where I focussed on my current case. I looked up Walton Endicott's number again and rang him, only to be greeted by his voicemail.

"I'm sorry, but I can't answer thy call reight now but if tha wants to leave thy number, I'll get back to thee t'minute I can."

A Haxforder through and through to judge from his thick brogue. I left my name and number and asked him to get in touch with me as soon as was convenient.

That done, I rang Georgie and asked for her sister's number.

"You're wasting your time, Christine."

"On the contrary. In this kind of inquiry, it's vital that we look at every aspect. I'm not accusing Karen, but I do need to talk to her. Now if you just give me her number, I can make arrangements to meet her, probably tomorrow."

She conceded defeat and dictated the number to

me. I cut the connection, punched the number into my mobile, put it to my ear, and waited.

"Karen Dawkins."

"Ah, Mrs Dawkins. It's Christine Capper. We met very briefly last night. I'm acting on behalf of your sister, and I really need to speak to you."

"Well, you can take a flying one can't you? I've got nothing to say to you."

"You might think that, but you'd be surprised at what I can learn from a brief chat, and I must tell you, I've been in touch with Sergeant Hiscoe this morning, and she's insisted that Georgie is their prime suspect in the death of Annie Endicott. I don't believe that. I think someone is trying to fit Georgie up, and although she insists it's not you, I don't believe that."

"Now listen—"

I cut her off. "I don't have time to listen right now. How about we meet at, say, half past nine tomorrow morning? Just say where."

She fumed for a moment, then gave way. "Haxford Health Spa. I'll be in the cafeteria, and trust me, I won't be alone."

I ignored the implicit threat in her final words. "Half past nine tomorrow, then. I'll look forward to seeing you."

I guessed that would be the most unpleasant call I had to make. My next one was to Haxford Fixers, where Dennis answered.

"What do you want this time?"

"To speak to Greg. Put him on, will you, Dennis?"

There was a slight delay, and I heard Dennis call across workshop. "Herriot. It's our lass. She wants to speak to you."

Another delay before Greg picked up the phone. "Christine?"

"Don't sound so surprised, Greg. I could speak to Dennis any time, but catching up with you guys is easier when you're at work. Patricia Keenan. You told me earlier that you knew her. Any danger you can tell me where she lives?"

"Tatton Street. It's just off the town centre, somewhere over the back of Weaver Street. Your satnav'll get you there. Don't know that you'll find her in at this hour. If she's not already out on the beer, it won't be long before she is."

"Tatton Street. You don't know what number?"

"I think it's number seven. In fact, I'm sure it is. But if she asks, I didn't tell you."

Another item ticked off my 'to do' list. In any inquiry there's a sort of lull in the early days while you're busy trying to sort out who to speak to and what questions you want to ask. Right now I was making tiny progress. An appointment with Karen Dawkins, my number left with Walt Endicott, and I knew where to find Patricia Keenan. All I had left to do was track down Heidi Flanagan.

Thoughts of Heidi and her acerbic opinion of the shakes, reminded me I had one in my bag. I'd had them before – usually store-bought – and they were tolerable. I can't remember whether I lost any weight using them.

Using my hand-held blender it took just a couple of minutes to drop the powder and mix it with 200ml of skimmed milk. Then I took a sample sip.

Dear me, it was absolutely awful. I hadn't tasted

anything that foul since the tea I made at Georgie's place earlier in the day. It was like drinking sludge. I wouldn't taste much of the flavour, Georgie had told me. She didn't have that quite right. I couldn't taste any of it. It was like drinking a glass of the mud which Cappy the Cat regularly brought home on his paws.

I threw the rest away.

I was tempted to ring Georgie again, but decided against it. She'd heard enough of me for one day. I could always call at the library first thing in the morning, where my good friend Kim Aspinall would track down Heidi Flanagan's address for me.

What was it some poet said about the best laid plans of timorous wee beasties? I was busy congratulating myself when the phone rang. Mandy.

I made the connection. "What can I do for you this bright and sunny afternoon?"

"You were at the Haxford Losers Club meeting last night. I'm just wondering if you'd come across a woman named Heidi Flanagan."

"Great minds thinking alike," I said. "I was about to start tracking her down tomorrow morning."

"Don't waste your time. She's dead."

Chapter Thirteen

I almost said, 'you're joking' but I knew Mandy better than that. She would not joke about anything so serious. "Poisoned?"

"Depends. If you consider the way blunt force trauma, getting her head smashed in, might poison her attitude to her killer, then yes, she was poisoned."

"When?"

"Too early to say, Chrissy. A neighbour had heard some kind of argument last night, couldn't get an answer this morning, and raised the alarm. When our people broke in, they found her in the living room, her head caved him. We think sometime last night, but as usual, were waiting for the pathologist. I rang you because I wondered whether you'd come across her and whether you could tell me anything about her."

"The bit that I know wasn't pleasant. She was simply attitude on legs." I risked a quick glance at my watch. "Half past five. Any chance you could meet me in the bar of the Tavern in, say, twenty minutes?"

"I'll be there. What do you want? Bacardi and whatever, gin and it, spritzer?"

"White wine spritzer. I'm on my way now."

The Tavern's full name was the Market Tavern,

standing at the rear of the market hall. A popular watering hole especially at the end of the working day, when people popped in for a quick one before making their way home, and when I got there, it was already quite crowded, and I found Mandy sat at a table in the far corner, reserving the only other seat for me.

The spritzer was more than welcome. But Mandy was in a business mood.

"Okey-dokey, you've got your snifter, what can you tell me about Mrs Flanagan?"

From there I gave her a detailed account of our two encounters last night, the one in the Haxford Losers Club when she demanded not only her money back but her membership dues, and later when she collared me as I climbed into my car outside the Barley Mow.

"Legend has it," I concluded, "that she was quite free with her favours, a consistent griper, and I did suspect that she might have been the one selling Georgie's member's details to Karen Dawkins. They were certainly friendly enough when I bumped into them at the bar. I'm seeing Dawkins first thing tomorrow morning so I'll give her a push on that. Oh, and Heidi also told me in a roundabout way that she'd had a bit of a thing with Jonathan Ambrose."

"So has half of Haxford according to rumour. Trouble is, Chrissy, you're approaching this from the point of view that says Georgie Tibbett is innocent. We're coming at it from the other side. We think she's guilty. Let's face it, two of her members, both known to be giving her grief, both killed yesterday. And all she told us under interview was that she's having a tough time of it lately. It was flak she could do without."

I nodded. "She told me the same thing. Even so, I don't believe it was her. Well, I don't believe it was her who poisoned Annie Endicott."

"What time did you leave her last night? Heidi Flanagan, I mean, not Georgie Tibbett?"

I had to think about the question. "Getting on for ten o'clock. She was alive and well then. She even tried to warn me off about Ambrose."

"Wanted more of him for herself?"

"Maybe but not according to him. When I spoke to Georgie this morning, she was very depressed and obviously she blamed you. Not exclusively, but you didn't help her situation. So what time did you let her go last night?"

"About ten o'clock. I did tell you first thing. It's perfectly feasible that she took a cab to the spa, picked up her car, and drove to Flanagan's place and confronted her. From there, an argument developed, and Georgie ended it when she battered the woman about the head."

I remained circumspect. "You're going to have to prove that, Mandy."

"I know, but right now we've got CSI going over Flanagan's house, and if we get one trace of Georgie Tibbett, we'll have her. All I want from you, Chrissy, is that you keep me up to speed with anything you learn."

"No problem. Any word on the poison that was used to kill the Endicott woman?"

"Not yet. You know what pathology and toxicology are like. You can't rush them. We should know tomorrow, and Flanagan's PM is schedule for tomorrow once they've done with Annie. I'll keep you posted."

During the short time I spent with Mandy, my phone rang twice, but both times, I ignored it. As I made my way back to the car, I checked the call menu and it was Walton Endicott both times.

Settling behind the wheel, I rang him.

"It's Christine Capper, Mr Endicott," I announced. "I rang earlier and you tried to get me a couple of times in the last, sort of, twenty minutes."

"Oh, Aye. What is it tha wants doing?"

"Nothing. Well, I'm not ringing for gardening services, although I might need you by the end of the summer. Fact is, I'm a private investigator and I'm ringing about your wife's untimely passing."

"Nay, lass. I've nowt to say about that. It's all down to that bag, Tibbett, and the cops are handling it."

"There's some doubt about that, Mr Endicott."

"Norrin my mind, there isn't. Capper, you say? Are you owt to do wi' Dennis Capper who works at Haxford Fixers?"

"He's my husband."

"Aye, and you're just as persistent as him, aren't ye? If tha wants to know owt, talk to the cops."

And with that, he cut the call off.

I drove home from the Tavern in a grim mood. Everything Mandy said made absolute sense, and yet something told me that it had little or nothing to do with Georgie. But it would be Thursday morning before I could do anything more about it.

Dennis was ahead of me for once, already home

when I got there, and asking, a) what was for tea and b) where had I been? The order of his questions demonstrated his absolute priorities. If I'd been out partying and come home with my underwear in my pocket, he'd still want to know what was for tea before asking what I'd been up to.

I served him a microwaved beef hotpot from the freezer while I settled for a jacket potato with grated cheddar, and while we ate, I told him of my day.

It takes a lot to make Dennis pause while eating, but my account of the day managed it.

"Hang on. I thought you were supposed to be chasing these people who're hassling Mam."

Even Cappy the Cat looked up. I don't know what it was about Dennis's words which made our finicky feline take notice, but I didn't really have the opportunity to consider it as Dennis railed on.

"That's to do with us, not a couple of old bats who've been topped."

"Dennis—"

"I mean, I thought we should take priority. Never mind making a few bob poking your nose in where it doesn't concern you. We should be looking out for Mam."

"Dennis—"

"And I thought you always got on all right with her. In fact, you always said that as mothers-in-law go, she is the best. It just goes to show—"

This time it was me interrupting him. "For God's sake just shut up and listen for a minute." When I had him listening, I went on. "Life would be a lot better if you paid me some attention now and then."

"I offered last night but you said you were too

tired."

I could feel my temper rising with every passing second. "That's not what I'm talking about. I'm talking about paying attention when I speak to you. I already told you that I'd spoken to the people at Foulsham. I have to call on Eunice tomorrow to get her documents, and I've arranged with her and them for me to deal with the matter, not you, not your mother, me. But as things stand, it is official. They are genuinely looking into your Uncle Billy's estate. It'll take months for them to sort it out, and there's nothing more I can do other than submit the necessary documents. Clear?"

"If you say so."

"I do. They're not hassling your mother. She is Billy's only surviving relative. Or at least, she's the only surviving relative at that level of the family tree. After her the only others are you, your brothers and sisters. So what is it you are asking of me? You want me to sit around twiddling my thumbs for the next nine months or a year waiting for them to deal with the matter?" I didn't wait for an answer. "Right. In the meantime, I have other work I need to concentrate on, particularly my efforts for Radio Haxford and the case of Georgie Tibbett accused of a murder she hasn't committed. Do we understand each other?"

"Yes." The word was snapped off, indicating that as far as he was concerned, the argument was done with.

But not for me. "Just so you know where you're up to, I have to go out early tomorrow morning. I have to see Karen Dawkins, Jonathan Ambrose,

Patricia Keenan, then your mother, I have to get the copying and scanning done for Eunice, and when that's done, I have to go to the police station and speak to Mandy. Right?"

"And I told you to keep away from Ambrose."

"I have no choice in the matter, but don't worry. I'll be wearing my cast iron drawers and a padlocked chastity belt. You know me better than that, and don't pretend you don't."

The argument set the tone for the evening. By eight o'clock, Dennis was in front of the television watching repeats of *Bangers & Cash* or *Top Gear* on the Freeview channels, and I settled down in the conservatory to watch the midsummer sunset, with my laptop focusing on various social media pages, seeking anything I might find on Heidi Flanagan.

It didn't take long.

She had accounts with all the major sites, including several dating sites, where she insisted she was not looking for marriage, just fun, a good time. On the major sites, she was a consistent gripe, complaining about everything from Westminster to Haxford Borough Council, our local shops to online shopping, and I could not find a single generous word about Haxford Losers Club. Quite the opposite.

Looking at her history, she'd been a member of Georgie's setup for over a year and from week one, she was carping, moaning, spitting blood and feathers, and generally declaring the entire exercise as a waste of her precious free time.

When you narrowed down the complaints, the cause of them seemed to be that there were so few male members (I use the word 'members' to mean men in general, not their other attributes). The one person she was interested in was Tel Wheatley, but he'd insisted he wasn't interested, and from there, she proceeded to slag him off as an over the hill, hick athlete, who was never any good on or off the football field.

While reading through this, I made a note to speak to Tel Wheatley tomorrow, or as soon as I could track him down.

Reading through this catalogue of bile, nowhere did she give any indication of a man – or woman for that matter – who really resented her so much that they would be willing to resort to murder, and when I checked out other social media accounts, Tel Wheatley, Georgie Tibbett, Karen Dawkins, even Jonathan Ambrose, none of them gave her so much as a mention. I could understand that from Ambrose's point of view. If what she told me was true, he would hardly be likely to shout, *I gave Heidi Flanagan a good seeing to and then dumped her* on social media pages, would he?

None of these people, and amongst that number I could include Patricia Keenan, ever gave her the time of day.

What was interesting was Keenan's account. Like Heidi, she was what could be termed man-mad, and most of her posts confirmed the opinion that Greg Vetch had given me. Most men might consider her easy prey, but in fact it was the other way round. She was the predator.

At half past ten, I decided I'd had enough. I shut the laptop down, shuffled through to the living room, told Dennis I was going to bed, and received a grunt in return. I could see it would be a silent breakfast the following morning. From there, I made myself a final couple of tea, and called it a night.

Chapter Fourteen

Thursday, June 22, the morning after the solstice, and every news and social media page on the web was crowing about the blazing sunshine and temperatures. Over breakfast of muesli and a cup of strong coffee, my gloomy thoughts settled around Annie Louise Endicott and Heidi Flanagan. Neither woman had lived to see the glory of Midsummer.

It's easy to sit in judgement on women whose behaviour did not come up to acceptable standards as defined by the mass opinions of social media, but no matter what their faults – and other than perfect specimens such as myself, we all have them – they still had a right to life. They had been robbed of that right, whether Mandy had it right and it was Georgie Tibbett, or I had it right and it was someone pointing the finger at Georgie Tibbett, made little difference other than to the person concerned. Whoever it was, the perpetrator should pay for his or her crimes.

As I predicted the previous evening, Dennis and I exchanged barely a single word before he left for work, leaving me to prepare for the day's hassles. I had two people yet to track down: Patricia Keenan and Tel Wheatley, and I had to deal with what would be an uncomfortable interview, perhaps confrontation, with Karen Dawkins, and I could see that might be complicated by the presence of Jonathan Ambrose. She did say she would not be alone, and it was odds on that Ambrose would be her witness.

The weather called for light attire, so while Cappy the Cat dealt with his morning duties, i.e. getting rid of the birds in the back garden, paying his morning call to the Timmins's back garden, and generally being as moody as he could, I put on a pair of jeans and a bland, pale yellow T-shirt, and with our crusty kitty safely indoors, I climbed into the car just after nine o'clock. Cappy the Cat was sat in the window, watching me drive away, and I could almost feel the angry laser beams blazing from his eyes and burning into me.

All windows open, sunroof raised, the sound of the Orchestral Manoeuvres in the Dark blaring from the speakers, I enjoyed a leisurely drive from Bracken Close to Wakey Moor and the health spa. Contrary to the depression settling over me when I first got out of bed, I was feeling quite relaxed.

It didn't last long. It never does.

I approached the reception desk and the fit-as-a-fiddle woman on duty, a prime example of tracksuit and administrative efficiency, declared, "Members only."

"I see. So, even if I'm here under invitation, I have no choice but to become a member. Is that correct?"

"I, er. I'm sorry, can we start again."

"Of course. My name's Christine Capper and I'm a presenter on Radio Haxford. Now I'm sure that Mr Fletcher Leeming would not want me to deliver a negative opinion to my listeners, would he?"

"I, er…"

"You do speak plain English, don't you? I only ask because your last two sentences have begun with 'I, er'. Or is it my Haxford accent that's putting you off?"

By now she was totally bewildered. "I'm sorry. Can we start again for the third time?"

I smiled encouragement, although I had an awful feeling that it came out as more like a sneer of triumph. "Right. I am Christine Capper. I have an appointment with Karen Dawkins. She runs the Haxford (not so) Heavies diet group, and she asked me to meet her in the cafeteria at half past nine." I checked my watch. "It's now 9:32, and you are making me late for my appointment."

"Hold on a moment." She picked up the telephone, muttered into it, then put the receiver down. "Ms Dawkins is waiting for you. You know where to go?"

The thought crossed my mind that I'd like to tell her where to go, but I acquiesced and assured her that I would find the place.

And it was not difficult. Through a set of double doors, it was there on my right, a large, spacious and modern cafeteria as befitted a health spa.

I couldn't say the same about the menu which offered plenty of healthy options, but beyond them you could indulge in anything and everything from a full English breakfast, to fish and chips, to a Sunday roast (on Sundays, obviously). I ordered a cup of coffee, scanned the thinly populated area, and spotted Karen Dawkins and, as I suspected, Jonathan Ambrose over by the window.

Over the years that I'd worked as a private investigator, I had been in this situation any number of times, but that did nothing to quell the butterflies in my tummy. People reacted in different ways, but the most consistent aspect was resentment, an attitude that asked who was this woman daring to ask them questions.

I recall my jitters at the prospect of meeting Ballinger and Petra Leach, but I prevailed over the situation by the simple use of plain speaking and common sense tinged with a little diplomacy of course.

This, I guessed, would be just as difficult. Both were dressed in what could be described as gym clothes: shorts, T-shirts, trainers. The shorts showed more of Karen Dawkins's chunky thighs than should be allowed at this hour, but on Ambrose they demonstrated exactly the opposite. Muscle packed legs. The same went for his arms, biceps bulging, sinewy wrists and large hands wrapped around a cup of tea or coffee. Karen's arms were bulging too, but it was more to do with flab than muscle.

The most awkward thing about the seating positions was they were opposite each other, and I really needed them all the same side of the table so I could face them. Not that anything I had to say was any business of Ambrose's, but it was almost inevitable that he would butt in, coming to her defence now and then.

I made my way over, and sat down alongside him, and moved my seat out slightly to put some space between us. I smiled on Karen. "Good morning, Ms Dawkins. Another beautiful day."

"Cut the crap and get on with it."

"I prefer to be laid-back, even when it comes to matters of business, but if that's your attitude, very well. Have the police been to see you yet?"

"They came to see us yesterday about Annie Endicott. I told them to get lost. I didn't know the woman, and her death had nothing to do with me."

"That would have been, when? Yesterday morning?"

"As a matter of fact, yes."

"Probably while I was speaking to your sister." I paused deliberately to ensure my next statement had maximum impact. "They haven't called to see you about Heidi Flanagan yet?"

Karen frowned and I cast a quick glance at Ambrose whose eyebrows rose.

"Heidi Flanagan?"

I kept my tones matter of fact. "Yes. She's dead."

Once again I paused, trying to judge the impact the announcement had on them. It was intriguing. Karen was shocked, Ambrose less so.

"She was beaten to death on Tuesday night, not long after I left the Barley Mow. I met with my good friend Mandy Hiscoe yesterday afternoon, and she's got her sights firmly fixed on Georgie." Another timely pause. "Me? I'm of a different opinion. I think someone is trying to set your sister up, and thinking about the civil war between you, you come top of the list."

That hit the spot as well as any Bacardi and coke after a hard day's work. Karen's features underwent a rapid change from shock to surprise to out and out anger.

"How dare you—"

"I used to be a cop," I interrupted. "That's how I dare."

"That doesn't give you the right to come here accusing Karen." The comment came from Ambrose, the first he had made.

I stared him in the eye. "So sue me. If you think I won't repeat what I've said to anyone else, you're mistaken. Given sufficient evidence, I will repeat it to Mandy Hiscoe and her team, and when it comes to gathering evidence, believe me, I'm top drawer. Your best option, Karen, is to speak to me, convince me that it is your sister and not you."

By this time, Karen was fuming. "It's not me. I just told you, I didn't know the Endicott woman, and I have absolutely no reason to murder Heidi Flanagan."

"No. Quite the opposite. She was the one feeding you information on Georgie's group, wasn't she?"

"Do you specialise in getting it wrong?"

The bitter, rhetorical question, came from Karen. Ambrose laughed.

I maintained my aplomb. "I do get it wrong now and again, but I am well known for getting to the core of these kinds of issues. Was Heidi Flanagan feeding you information regarding Georgie's group?"

"No, she bloody well wasn't. Jonathan told you that in the Barley Mow the other night. You want to know the truth, Mrs private eye, nobody was feeding me any information on Georgie's shambles. People were leaving her group and joining mine for the simple reason that the garbage she served doesn't work."

"You're talking about the diet shakes?"

"Yes."

Having sampled one the previous afternoon, I could understand why it didn't work, but I wasn't about tell Karen that. "Georgie says different."

"I know she does, and we've had this argument a dozen ways from Sunday." Karen fumed silently for a moment. "All this is because she dropped Jonathan, Brian left her, and Jonathan moved in with me. That's it. Aside from that, I have no problem with my sister. I'll tell you something else, too. The only thing I'll agree with you about is that she did not kill Endicott and she did not kill Heidi Flanagan."

This came as a bit of a surprise, but I hid it. "Well, at least we have some common ground. What makes you so sure? I mean, let's be honest about this, I had a long conversation with her yesterday, and she's very depressed. According to her, she's at rock bottom, she's got nowhere else to go other than up or to prison, the way she talked, it sounds like she prefers prison."

Karen looked through the windows, out on the sunshine blessing the surrounding moorland. When she turned back to face me, she was much calmer.

"She doesn't have the capacity to kill anyone. Yeah, like me, she's a snapper, but there's a difference between shouting your mouth off, and lamping someone. She's not violent. Neither am I."

I aimed a finger at Ambrose. "According to him, she punched you."

"She slapped me. That was all. And she apologised right away."

"Perhaps she apologised to Annie and Heidi after

she'd killed them."

"It wasn't her, it wasn't me."

"But obviously it was someone," I said. "Someone who felt strongly enough about Heidi Flanagan to batter her about the head, until she was dead. I don't believe it's Georgie, and if I take your insistence as the gospel, then it's not likely to be you. So who?" I turned my attention on Ambrose. "You?"

There was no humour in his response. "Unlike Karen and Georgie, I have been known to strike out at people, as you're likely to find out if you accuse me again."

"Don't threaten me, Mr Ambrose. You were quite scathing about Mrs Endicott when I spoke to you a couple of nights ago, and Heidi Flanagan's opinion of you wasn't particularly charitable."

"I don't care about other people's opinions, Mrs Capper. Heidi Flanagan could think whatever she pleased. I didn't know the woman well, and whatever she told you, was based purely on our occasional, informal conversations at the bar of the Barley Mow."

"According to Heidi, her opinion of you was based on something rather more horizontal." Before he could react, I redirected the conversation. "Tell me about Patricia Keenan."

"Another one who's only happy when she's laid under some man," Karen said. "She's had a string of affairs since she and her husband split up. Tel Wheatley was one of them."

"She didn't get on too well with Heidi."

"Direct competition."

That was Karen speaking again. I looked to

Ambrose for confirmation and he shrugged.

"I don't know why you're looking at me. Whatever she told you, it was a lie. She might have – dare I say – fancied me, but she never came on to me and I never hit on her."

I drank my coffee. "All right. We'll leave it at that, but just be aware that Mandy Hiscoe is now looking into two deaths, but both connected to the Haxford Losers Club, and she will want to speak to you. I'll bid you both good day."

"Just a minute."

Once again it was at Karen's insistence, and I sat down. "What is it?"

"You spoke to Georgie yesterday. You're making inquiries on her behalf. I know you private eyes. You don't work for nothing. How is she paying you?"

"The honest truth? She isn't. We have an arrangement whereby if I can demonstrate her innocence, I'll arrange an interview on Radio Haxford. Either that or I'll get her to sponsor my vlog for a month. I don't normally do charity work, Karen, but I feel that in Georgie's case, she needs help."

"You're right," Karen agreed. "Let me give you the bottom line on everything. Georgie and I had a good beat on things when we were running the diet group together. I led the groups because I'm better in front of people, but Georgie is a qualified food scientist and technologist. She baked the diet biscuits we sold to the group. What am I saying, she baked? She's still baking them for me. Or at least she was up to yesterday. The money I pay her and the pennies she makes from the Losers Club, are her only income. If the filth – pardon my local bias – have shut down the manufacturing process, she's got nothing coming in."

"Yes. I went through this with Georgie yesterday. Well, most of it. She didn't tell me that she was still baking biscuits for you, but she did stress that she's broke. According to her, it's only a matter of time before the bank foreclosures on her mortgage."

"Well, I didn't know she was that close. But it just goes to show you how we don't speak to each other as much as we should. So let me strike a deal with you. How much would you charge me for proving Georgie's innocence?"

"Thirty pounds an hour, and I charge a basic retainer of sixty pounds, the price of two hours' work. I've already put in more than that, but if we start with a clean sheet, and you're really serious about taking me on, then that's the deal."

Without further ado she reached for her purse, opened it, pulled out three twenties, and pushed them across the table to me.

Ambrose baulked. "Just a minute, Karen. Are you sure you know what you're doing?"

"She's my sister. What do you want me to do, Jon? Leave her to rot in prison? See her on the stret, move into a homeless hostel, creditors chasing her for the rest of her life?" She switched her attention to me. "You need some kind of a contract signing?"

More than happy with the outcome, I said, "I do, but it's not critical. I can catch you any time within the next couple of days, and I will be round and about chasing up other potential leads." I got to my feet. "Thank you for your help. Both of you. I'll get on with the job."

Chapter Fifteen

As I left the cafeteria I glanced back to see Karen and Ambrose in a heated discussion. I couldn't hear what was being said, but there were a lot of gestures from Ambrose. I remember what Sandra Limpkin said to me the previous day about how he preferred his women a) under him and b) with a healthy purse from which he could help himself. I guessed that he was none too happy with Karen engaging me to clear her sister's name. It would be taking funds away that he might have hoped to milk.

Of course, it was all very well for Sandra to accuse him, and for me to speculate on the same, but could I find confirmation anywhere? Patricia Keenan, for example?

Right there and then, however, I had other matters on my mind. As I climbed into the car, I rang Eunice and asked her if she had the documents ready. She did, so I told her I would be there in ten minutes to collect them. From her place, I would make my way to CutCost, pick up some bits of shopping, and then have the documents scanned and saved to a memory stick in their photographic department.

As I made my way into Haxford and round to Jutland Mount, I had to wonder why they still called it a photographic department. Who used film in this day and age? A few stick-in-the-mud buffs, I should imagine, but by and large, that kind of anorak tended to develop the negatives and prints in their own darkrooms. The staff in photographic shops, such as the franchise in CutCost, passed most of their time scanning and printing documents from computers. True, they sold frames and were quite happy to set up any photograph to fit whatever frame the buyer wanted, but it was still computerised.

And it was just as well, I decided, when I arrived at the shop at a little after eleven o'clock, and met with an assistant who struggled to understand exactly what I wanted.

"People don't normally frame their birth and marriage certificates, Madam," she told me.

"I don't want them framing. I want them scanned and saved as jpegs to this memory stick." I held up the offending item.

"I'll have to scan the memory stick for viruses and stuff," she warned me.

I gave her my sweetest smile. "Be my guest."

The process took a little over fifteen minutes. No problem scanning and saving Eunice's council tax bill, which served as proof of her address, but getting the birth and marriage certificates down to a reasonable size which would fit in one readable image each, proved quite a task, but in the end the young woman presented me with the memory stick, the documents, and a bill for slightly under two pounds.

I spent another twenty minutes wandering round the store picking up a few bits and pieces: bread, potatoes, green vegetables, and essentials like eyeliner, mascara, eye-shadow, lipstick, foundation and other makeup, before hitting the homewares department and choosing my wallpaper.

Dennis often complained that when it came to making up my mind on stuff like that, I would dither for hours. He would have been proud of me this time. It took less than ten minutes to choose the correct paper and shade. Mind, he wouldn't be so pleased at the price. Just shy of £16 per roll, but it was what I wanted in the colour I preferred. A sort of silvery-white, decked with drawings of different cups for different coffees: cappuccino, latte, espresso and so on. I wasn't a big coffee drinker, I preferred tea, but I couldn't find paper with Darjeeling, Assam, Lapsang Souchong etc. and I couldn't see one with PG Pyramids, Typhoo One-Cup and what have you.

Happy with my morning's work so far, I climbed into my car and sat twiddling my thumbs as I tried to decide where to go next.

I could leave it to Dennis to return the documents to Eunice, and that allowed me to concentrate on the issue of Georgie Tibbett and the deaths of Annie Endicott and Heidi Flanagan.

Patricia Keenan and Tel Wheatley were both on my list of people to speak to, but before I left the car park, I rang Mandy.

"No news at this end," she reported. "Do you know anything more?"

"The only thing I know for sure is that Karen has hired me to prove her sister's innocence. On that basis, I don't think Karen would have killed these two women either."

"I know you better than that, Chrissy. If you're

right, and as far as I'm concerned it's a big if, then you must have at least one suspect."

"Jonathan Ambrose."

She chuckled. "And that's nothing to do with the fact that you don't like beefcake in general and him in particular?"

I laughed with her. "When have I ever been biased?"

"I can't remember, but I'll bet Paddy will remember a few incidents when he gets here later this afternoon."

I tutted. "He's taking control, is he?"

"It was odds-on. Two murders in less than forty-eight hours? Definitely a Paddy job. Listen, girl, I'll have to shoot off. Things to do, people to hassle. You know the score. Keep me primed on anything you learn."

"Will do, as long as you promise to keep Paddy off my back."

"Deal."

So far so good. All I had to do now was decide between Patricia Keenan and Tel Wheatley. It was no contest. I had an address for Keenan, I had no clue where I would find Wheatley.

I called up Tatton Street on the satnav. Simple enough. It was, as Greg Vetch told me, in a clutch of streets behind Weaver Street, home of the Engine House pub, Lester Grimes's favourite watering hole, and I knew exactly the route to take me there.

It's surprising how quickly time goes on, especially when you're hassling with the traffic on the Haxford town centre bypass. It was almost half past twelve when I turned into Tatton Street, and parked opposite number seven.

The houses in this part of town were the older ones, the places which harked back to the days when the Haxford economy relied on the woollen mills. Brick built rows of terraced houses, two bedrooms, two downstairs rooms, outside lavatory. Most of them had been suitably modernised and boasted central heating and an interior bathroom, but the only way you could squeeze the bathroom into the available space was by shrinking one of the upstairs bedrooms. I knew about these houses. I grew up in one and my parents still lived there.

I locked the car (whenever you parked in the vicinity of the Engine House, you always locked your car) crossed the street, and rang the doorbell.

A minute later, the woman appeared. I didn't know who she was, but she wasn't Patricia Keenan.

"Oh. I'm sorry to disturb you. I was looking for Mrs Keenan."

"Well, you're looking in the wrong place. She lives at number twenty-seven, and as far as I know, she hasn't been a Mrs for years."

I apologised again, climbed back in the car, and drove further up the street.

The house was no different to any of the others, and I hoped that the brusque woman I'd disturbed, had it right.

She did. I barely knocked on the door, when it flew open and an angry Patricia Keenan glared down at me. "What do you want?"

This kind of irritable greeting always brought out the worst in me. For a moment I was tempted to reply, 'Well, it's been a good few years since me and my old man could make the car springs rock, and I was hoping you might give me a few pointers,' but of course, I lacked the temerity, the sheer neck to say anything so crass. I cleaned it up a little, and said, "For all you know, I might be looking for the secret of your success with men."

"Get stuffed."

She made to close the door but I put my foot in it, much to my dismay when she slammed it on my toe.

She opened it and raised her voice. "What the hell do you want?"

"A toe that isn't bruised," I told her. "Other than that, I want to speak to you regarding Annie Endicott and Heidi Flanagan."

"I've nowt to say to you, so—"

I cut her off. "The alternative is you speak to the police. It won't take five minutes to get Mandy Hiscoe here."

That did the trick. She backed off, fully opened the door, and said, "You'd better come in. I'm not putting on free entertainment for the neighbours."

She led me into a simply (cheaply) furnished front room where she sat near the fire while I perched on the settee in the corner furthest from her. Putting aside the inevitable question of why anyone would want to switch on the fire when the outside temperature was enough to start the blaze without any help, I remembered the way she had confronted Heidi Flanagan two nights ago and with an aching toe to remind me, I didn't trust this woman not to turn violent.

Sitting down, kicking off my shoe. Lifting my foot and rubbing at the injured digit, I happened to glance at the blank television on its glass table and I noticed a wrapper. Pale blue, small and oblong, I had to strain my neck to read the legend, *Haxford (not so) Heavies*, and I'm sure she noticed my interest, but by then it was too late for her to remove it.

I put that issue to one side and asked, "You've heard about Heidi?"

She nodded. "I've heard. Nothing to do with me. I couldn't stand the woman."

"I think everyone realised that on Tuesday night. But the police are looking for the killer. Having seen the way you and her almost came to blows, I figured you were a good candidate."

"Get out."

"When I have the answers to some questions."

"Do I have to throw you out?"

"Try, but just remember, I used to be a police officer. And even with a potentially broken toe, I know how to look after myself."

"So do I."

Impasse. Neither of us disposed to move.

In the end I had to back off a little. "We're getting off on the wrong foot, Patricia." Mention of the wrong foot reminded my big toe that it still hurt and I rubbed at it again. "Let me explain my position. The police are convinced that Georgie Tibbett killed both Annie and Heidi. I think she's innocent, and if you've heard of me, if you know anything about me, you'll know that I don't rest until I pin down the real criminal. I'm not saying it's you. You're just one person the police will eventually want to speak to. All I'm seeking is whatever information you can give me about the circle of people involved in the two diet clubs."

She too took a step down from her confrontational stance. "There's not much I can tell you, really. Heidi was a tart. Anything in pants was her preference. And she never had a good word to say about them before or after. Pretty much the same as Endicott, except that Annie kept her knickers on. I'm divorced, and yeah, I like a good time. I had a bit of a thing with Tel Wheatley a while back, and the minute she found out about that, Heidi went after him. He told her exactly where she could go. Result, she slagged Tel off something awful on a few social media channels. That's how she was. And even if she had got her way, she would still have slagged him off."

"You were quick to confront her on Tuesday night."

"Because that's how it was between us. Trust me, if I'd have spoken up first, she wouldn't have waited to have a go back. I never had any time for her, even when we were at school."

I recalled that Patricia had indeed spoken first, but I decided not press it. "You were at school together?"

"Over thirty years ago, but yeah, we went to Haxford comprehensive. I'm about three or four months younger than her, but we were in the same year at school. I'm telling you something, Mrs private eye, if you're looking for anyone prepared to top her, you'll have a queue from here to Huddersfield and back."

"Yes, well, I'm afraid I see things differently. I don't care how bad someone is, they still have a right to life. Even if you're going to lock them up for the rest of that life, no one has the right to take it away."

Now that I had some circulation back in my foot, I stood up and put my shoe on. "I can't think of anything else I need to know right now, but you should be aware that the police will probably visit you in the next day or two. Oh, while I think on, can you tell me where I might find Tel Wheatley?"

She glanced at the clock on the mantelpiece. "At this hour, he'll be in the bar of the Engine House. He likes his pop, and that's what finished us."

Along with Lester Grimes. I couldn't stop the thought from entering my head.

As I prepared to leave, I looked again at the biscuit wrapper, confirmed my earlier observation, and pointed at it. "You're a devotee of Karen Dawkins as well as Georgie Tibbett, are you?"

"No. Not particularly. I just need to lose a bit of weight. Now that Georgie's out of the scene, I do what I have to."

I gave her a grudging 'thank you', left the house, climbed into my car, and drove back through the latticework of streets to the Engine House.

It was known locally as the Sump Hole largely because a mill had once stood nearby and rumour had it that the pub was situated where the boiler house, which ran the mill's machinery, once stood. The fact that the pub claimed to be there in the early eighteen hundreds and the mill wasn't demolished until just after the end of the second world war never seemed to cross anyone's mind, least of all the bar's patrons.

And one of those patrons, as if you didn't already know, was Lester Grimes, the seriously junior partner at Haxford Fixers. He sometimes complained that he didn't make as much money out of the business as Dennis, Tony, and now Greg, but as always, there was a simple explanation: he didn't put in the same hours as they did.

It was no surprise, therefore, when I bumped into Lester as I walked in.

"Hey up, it's cuddly Chrissy. What you doing here, lass? Playing away from home while Dennis is grafting his n… grafting?"

"I'm working, Lester, and shouldn't you be?"

"I am working, I needed some bits and bobs for the job I'm doing, and as you know, I don't drive no more, so thought I'd have a liquid lunch while I were out."

It was an old tale, pulled for drinking and driving, he was fined and banned and decided that in a toss-up between his car and the beer, Haxford Best Bitter was more important to him.

"Any danger of a lift back to t'mill?"

"Yes, if you want to hang on half an hour while I speak to Tel Wheatley. But won't Dennis have something to say?"

"What? You're only giving me a lift."

"I meant about you being AWOL from work."

"Hey, I'm a partner, not a skivvy. I don't tell your Cappy when he can come and go, so he can say what he likes. Besides, you'll need me here to look after you. There's some rough sorts in this pub."

I laughed. "None rougher than you, Lester. Now come on. Show me where I can find Tel Wheatley."

"He'll be in the tap room playing darts."

Chapter Sixteen

There was an air of silence in the back room while Tel Wheatley's opponent, a man of about forty wearing the overalls of a local construction company, was throwing. According to my arithmetic the numbers on the chalkboard indicated that Tel needed 75 to take the game, while the builder needed 167.

"You has to leave your phone off or in flight doings," Lester whispered as we made our way in. "If someone bells you, and you puts the players off, they'll chuck you out."

A man next to him nudged Lester and in a similar low voice, urged, "Button it, Grimy."

Never one to back off easily, Lester leaned into him. "You too, Snoggy."

I wondered about the curious nickname, various, gregarious, not very pleasant images rushing into my mind. Ignoring it, I followed Lester's advice and switched my phone into flight mode. Then I focussed on the man. I was sure I recognised him. I tapped him on the shoulder and as he faced me, I realised it was Barry Snodgrass. When he saw me, he gave me a weak smile and turned his attention back to the darts. This was his idea of getting the materials together for my kitchen?

I forgot about it for the time being and watched

the game. I didn't know all the ins and outs of darts. I know you started with a score of 501, and you had to get down to zero, but you had to finish precisely on zero. If you needed, say, twenty-five, and you scored twenty-six, then hard lines. You had to go again – when it was your turn, obviously. I also knew that you had to finish on a double. Tel's opponent managed to score a hundred by hitting treble twenty, then twenty twice again, and it left him needing sixty-seven to win.

There was a murmur of appreciation when he stepped back to let Tel play. During this brief impasse, Lester whispered again. "Tel'll probably play fifteen, top, and double top for the game."

I wasn't exactly sure what top and double top meant, but it soon became clear when Tel's first dart landed in fifteen, his second in twenty, and his third struck double twenty. A muted cheer went up around the room, the two men shook hands, and I noticed the builder pass a fiver to Tel.

What surprised me more than Tel's skills of the game was the speed at which Lester worked out a total of seventy-five in the precise order which it came. Dennis was very good with numbers, especially if you put a pound sign in front of them, but I'd always figured that Lester's mental arithmetic was often clouded by excess Haxford Best Bitter. Obviously not when it came to a game of darts, and the reason soon became clear, when Barry surreptitiously handed a fiver to Lester.

I put on a frown of disapproval for Lester's benefit. "You were betting on Tel Wheatley?"

"He's red hot with the arrows, is Tel. Wise men

don't bet against him, but I wouldn't call Snoggy wise."

"How did he get the nickname? His real name is Barry Snodgrass."

"Oh, you know him, do you? He got his name same as I got mine. My name's Grimes so I'm Grimy. His name is Snodgrass so he's called Snoddy, but I prefer Snoggy. It winds him up more."

"He's painting and tiling our kitchen."

"Trust me, Chrissy, he'll do you a good job."

"If he ever gets a move on."

Another couple, a man and a woman this time, took to the mat for another game. I reached through the crowds, tapped Tel Wheatley on the shoulder, and whispered, "Any chance I could have a word, Mr Wheatley?"

He glared. "Now? Only there's a game on."

"I need to speak to you before the police get here." I was satisfied by the look of alarm on his face. "Annie Endicott and Heidi Flanagan." I said it a little too loud and received a couple of stares from the players and a number of people shushing me.

I turned my way back through the crowds, out into the comparative freedom of the main bar. When I checked, Tel Wheatley had followed me.

He signalled the barmaid for a drink, and she obviously knew his preference because she placed a pint glass under the lager pump and then looked at me. I ordered a sparkling water.

"Right. What are you on about?"

"Have you heard about Heidi?"

"I heard. It's nothing to do with me."

The barmaid placed his lager and my water on the

bar, held out her hand, and before I could reach into my purse, Tel handed over the five pounds he'd won in the game of darts.

When I had his full attention again, I told him, "Every time I speak to someone from Haxford Losers Club, I get the same nonsense. Nothing to do with me. First off, I didn't say it was anything to do with you, second whatever's going on, it is to do with the Losers Club, and right now I'm gathering information on Georgie Tibbett's behalf. The police say she did it, I say she didn't. I simply want to know what you know about the background. Is that asking too much?"

He sipped the head off the lager, looked around the room, spotted an empty table by the door, and nodded in that direction. He led, I followed, and I noticed he sat with his back to the door, almost as if he was ready to run for it should the need arise. I tucked in on the bench seat opposite him.

"Do you understand racism, Mrs Capper?"

The relevance of his question was a mystery, but at least he remembered who I was. "Not from experience, no, but if it's any consolation to you, I don't approve."

"I was born here in Haxford. I grew up here, I went to school here, I learned my skills in the building trade and on the football field right here. I have plenty of mates. But I also picked up plenty of enemies, and most of them take against me for one reason only." He ran both hands down his body from shoulder to hip. "The colour of my skin."

I said nothing. It was, of course, thoroughly reprehensible, and in this enlightened day and age, you'd think it belonged in the past, but it was still… Not exactly prevalent, but it was there.

"You're a builder?"

"A brickie by trade."

"There seem to be quite a few of them in here today."

"Shows you how bad things are, doesn't it." Another sip of lager and he went on. "I got into my fair share of scraps at school, I had more than my fair share of comments passed on the football field, especially from opponents when I scored against them. I'm out of work right now, looking round for site work or jobbing work, but everywhere I apply, there's nothing doing. And what will I get for that? I get called a lazy black… You can choose whatever offensive name you want to follow lazy and black."

I played with my wedding and engagement rings. "I'm sorry. There's no excuse for it." An idea occurred to me. "Would you be prepared to talk about it on radio?"

"How do you mean?"

"The Christine Capper Interview," I told him. "I did say the other night… Well, Georgie did. I'm a radio presenter as well as a private investigator. I do the agony aunt spot in the middle of Reggie Monk's show every Tuesday morning, and I also do occasional, in-depth interviews. Your experiences, Tel, would make a fascinating programme. I'm sure I can get the go ahead from my producer."

"And do you think that'll do any good?"

"We're local, not national, so we're hardly likely to make Westminster sit up and listen. But we do have a sizeable audience, and my show gets plenty of listeners. Come on, Tel. You have legitimate complaints about the way you've been treated over the years. Go public on them."

He hesitated for a moment. "I could think about it, sure. Would I get to meet your boss beforehand?"

"I'll arrange it." I switched tack. "On other matters, I'm not a football fan, but if it's any consolation to you, when you played for Haxford, I thought you were brilliant, I was surprised when you didn't move to Huddersfield or Sheffield."

He tapped his temple. "Bad attitude. Not focused enough. I liked my Friday nights out on the pop and the pull. I was an idiot. I know that now. Pity I didn't realise it at the time."

"I understand all this, but I don't see what any of it has to do with the murders of Annie Endicott and Heidi Flanagan."

"First, the filth. I'm black, so as far as they're concerned, it has to be me what done them."

I shook my head. "I used to be a police officer. I don't really believe that."

"You wouldn't because you haven't been through it, but trust me, it happens. Beyond that, when I said to you it's nothing to do with me, that comes from years of harassment, again because of my skin colour. I don't get involved in anything, Mrs Capper. Religion, politics, nothing at all. Annie-Lou and Heidi have been wasted. Tough. I'm sorry about that. But it wasn't me and I refuse point-blank to get involved."

I could see his point of view, but even so it was not what I wanted. "Let's reset, Tel. I'm not asking you to get involved, but I'm certain that somewhere along the line, Mandy Hiscoe and her people will want to speak to you. They're pursuing Georgie, I think they're wrong, I'm being paid to find the truth. It's as simple as that. I'm just looking into the background to find out who might be responsible. Just tell me, was there any undercurrent, undertone which might lead us in a specific direction?"

"You mean apart from Georgie's habit of screaming at everyone? Tons of it. Nobody liked nobody else, excepting maybe me and Trisha Keenan. We had a bit of thing a while back."

"I know. She told me. She said it was your drinking which finished it."

"She never mentioned her habit of putting the booze away then?"

I mentally kicked myself in the behind. When would I ever learn to keep my mouth shut?

"We're going round in circles here, Tel. According to the police, Annie Endicott was poisoned. Ignore Georgie for a moment and tell me who else would know about poisons?"

He chuckled. "Anyone who's ever read any Agatha Chris… Hang on. I'll tell you who does, but he didn't have nothing to do with the diet groups. Wally Endicott."

I noticed his brow was bathed in sweat. It was hot in that crowded pub but I hadn't yet begun to sweat. Was it the heat, combining with the excess weight he carried? Or was it the guilt of trying to point a finger away from him?

I took a glug of water to ease my parched throat, put the glass down, and shook my head. "I've already discussed that with the police and they've eliminated him… almost."

"No. You don't understand. Listen, I worked on that site when they were building the spa, and Wally came in as part of the council team to help clear the surrounding land. He might only be a gardener, but he doesn't half know his stuff, and back then, he was complaining about poisonous flowers in the moors and woods round the place. These days, he has the contract to keep the spa grounds tidy. He's there… what… at least two days a week. Less in the winter, obviously. Even now, he's forever complaining to Leeming, the general manager, about poisonous plants on the perimeter, where it all meets the moorland. I'm not saying he poisoned his missus – though I have to say, if she'd been my wife, I would have done – but there must be plenty of people at the spa who've heard him complaining to Leeming."

This was an entirely new angle, although it needed to be treated with caution. A lot depended on what the post mortem said with regard to Annie's poisoning.

"You don't know what sort of poisonous plants?"

He shrugged. "Haven't a clue."

I made a mental note to ring Mandy, see if she had the PM report yet, and beyond that, I needed to nag Walton Endicott again. A quick word with Fletcher Leeming wasn't out of the question either.

I wasn't yet finished with Tel Wheatley. "You were quick to stop Patricia Keenan tackling Heidi the other night. Is that because of your relationship with Patricia or because you don't like Heidi? And before you answer, Tel, I already know Heidi tried to seduce you at least once, and according to my information, you gave her the brush off."

"And did Trisha tell you how Heidi slagged me off on all of her social media accounts? You wanna know about my attitude to her? I couldn't stand the bloody woman. Did I kill her? No. End of story. She left the Barley Mow straight after you the other night then came back in with Leeming. I stayed while about eleven o'clock, got a taxi home, and I stayed there for the rest of the night. And no, I don't have no witnesses. You'll just have to take my word for it."

I delivered a weak half smile. "It's not me you have to convince. It's the police because they will get round to you. In the meantime, thanks for your help. I'll chase those leads up. And oh, you can expect a call from Eric Reitman, my producer at Radio Haxford."

From the table, I made my way through to the crowded back room, where the woman contestant had just beaten her male opponent on the dartboard, and Lester was busy collecting another three or four fivers.

I perched myself next to Barry Snodgrass and before I could say anything, he whispered, "I've got everything I need for your kitchen. Did you get the paper?"

"It's in the boot of my car."

"I'll be with you half eight tomorrow morning. One thing. It's Friday. Will you want me to work over the weekend? It's the missus you see. She nags me to take her out unless I'm working."

Curious. I did the same with Dennis. I threw the ball back in his court. "That's up to you, Barry. Does it cost more?"

"Another fifty."

"That's fine. You'll be finished, when? Sunday?"

"Possibly Saturday, but yeah, more likely Sunday."

"Great I'll see you tomorrow." As Lester passed, I tapped him on the arm. "If you want a lift back to the mill, I'm leaving now."

"Right with you, Chrissy."

A few minutes later, we were settled in my car and on the way to Haxford Mill.

"Did you make much money?" I asked.

"Put it this way. I've sunk a couple of pints, and I'm still twenty-five dabs in front. You see, Chrissy, it's all about knowing your people. Tel might not be a pro, but I've seen him play often enough to know that if he got off the beer, he could be. And Sally, the lass chucking the arrows in that last game, used to play for the county."

"And other people don't know that?"

"The ones I bet with didn't." He cackled to himself. "They were so sure that that geezer would win because he was so much taller."

"I swear that if you weren't an electrician you'd be an expert crook."

We got to the mill about fifteen minutes later, and out of pure courtesy, I went into the workshop along with Lester, just to say hello to everyone.

"Hey up, lass," Dennis greeted me. "I'm glad you're here. I've had a call from them, er, barbers or whatever they're called."

"Barbers?" I wondered whether Dennis had enjoyed a liquid lunch too.

"You know. Them as is hassling Mam."

"Dennis, they're heir hunters."

"I knew it had something to do with your rug."

"The word heir is spelt different. H-E-I-R as opposed to H-*A*-I-R and the H is silent, so it's pronounced 'air' as in the air we breathe. It's someone who is due to inherit."

"Whatever. Anyway they wanted to know about you."

I nodded. "Understandable. They're probably just confirming I am who I say I am. I'll be sending copies of your mother's documents off once I get home. In fact, while I think on, I've already got them saved to a memory stick. Can you take the stuff back to Eunice?"

"It's all official, then?"

Now I tutted. "I told you yesterday, Dennis, that it is all official. It'll take a long time to sort out, but when it does Billy's estate will come to Eunice. If she should pass away before then, it'll be distributed according to her will, so when you take the documents back tell Eunice, she must make a will out."

"I think she already has. Gimme the documents, I'll call on my way home."

A few minutes later, after leaving Eunice's correspondence with him, I climbed into the car, and spent a moment or two deciding which way to go, and then opted to head for home.

I had a couple of people to see yet, including the aforementioned Fletcher Leeming, but like Walton Endicott, he would be a busy man, and I'd probably have to make an appointment. Little or no point calling on Mandy. She probably didn't know any more, and whatever she did, she could tell me over the phone. And of course, I would need to speak to Eric about a potential interview with Tel Wheatley.

A light, late lunch, an hour's sleep, and a few phone calls sounded like the perfect afternoon.

Some chance. I was driving up Moor Road, within a couple of hundred yards of home, when my phone rang. Already on hands-free, I made the connection. "Christine Capper."

"Christine? It's Georgie Tibbett. I've been arrested again."

Chapter Seventeen

The right turn into Bracken Close was fifty yards ahead. With a wary eye on the roads, ensuring I had full control of the car, I asked, "Are you sure you've been arrested, Georgie? Or have you been taken in for questioning regarding Heidi Flanagan?"

"Doesn't seem to make a lot of difference to me. I'm with some nurk called Quinn, and he's locking me up until they've done fitting me up with both Annie and Heidi."

"Is Paddy there?"

"No. I'm with a policewoman called Suleman."

I turned into our street and cruised along, coming to a stop outside my house. "Put Rehana on, will you?"

There was a brief delay before Rehana Suleman spoke. "Hiya, Chrissy. Before you ask, I can't tell you anything."

"I know you can't, Rehana, but you could do me a favour. Tell Paddy Quinn I'm on my way to the station, and I have other information for him."

"I'll pass it on."

"Thanks. And can I speak to Georgie again?"

The phone changed hands once more.

"Georgie, I'm on my way to the station, I'll speak to Paddy when I get there. No guarantee that they'll let you go home but I do have some information which might make him think twice."

"Thanks, Chrissy. Karen rang me earlier today, and she told me she's hired you. I don't know how I'll pay her back."

"We have an agreement, yes, but now's not the time for you to be worrying about money. I'll ring off, get myself down there."

Killing the call, I reversed into the drive, and pulled straight back out, zoomed along the street, turned left on Moor Road, heading for the town centre. A glance at my fuel gauge told me I would need petrol very soon, so as I battled with the 2:30 traffic and the beginnings of the school run, I decided that when I was done with the police station, I'd go to Radio Haxford, get a word with Eric, and from there I would go to CutCost, fill the petrol tank, and deal with our weekly shop.

As I anticipated, Paddy was not in the best frame of mind when he came out to see me in reception. It was not as bad as it had been in the past, but that was down to a number of incidents, not least of which was helping pinpoint the real culprit in the Prater case, and handling the problems at Christmas Manor when blizzards prevented the police getting there.

Nevertheless, he was still far from pleased to see me. "Chrissy, when will you learn to keep your nose out of police investigations?"

"When people stop hiring me to poke my nose in, Paddy. I'm not saying you've got it wrong about Georgie, and I know you have to question her, but I have information which might throw a different light on the entire issue."

He sighed. "Always the bloody same."

"Yes, but that's because I don't run on rails. I ask the kind of questions that you people don't bother to ask. But first, let me ask you a question. Do you know what was used to poison Annie Endicott?"

"All we know for sure is that she was poisoned. The pathologist is leaning towards a substance called aconite."

"I don't know much about it, so I'm talking right off the top of my head, but Annie's husband, Walt, was forever warning the management at Haxford Health Spa about potentially poisonous plants growing on the perimeter of the site. Is aconite derived from plants?"

"How the hell should I know? I'm a detective, not a chemist."

"It's a question you could try asking Georgie. She does have a degree in food science, and it's a safe bet that she'll know about poisons derived from plants. I still have to talk to Walt Endicott, and I'll be going to see Fletcher Leeming, the spa manager. My information is that he knew about these plants."

"If that's so, we'll need to speak to him."

I giggled. "Bet I get there before you."

"Sod off." Another sigh escaped his lips. "You do whatever you think you have to do, Chrissy, but you know the rules. If you find anything out, you must tell us."

"Cross my heart and hope I can resist when some super stud movie star tries to sweep me off my feet."

That actually raised the slightest of smiles from him.

"Paddy, I don't want to be a total nuisance, but I

have to nip over to Radio Haxford. I promise I won't be any longer than, say, half an hour. Can I leave my car here for now?"

"You don't half know how to trespass on my goodwill, don't you? Yeah, all right. But I want it shifted by half past three. Okay?"

I gave him a smile by return. "Have I ever told you how much I love you?"

The reason I asked was down to Haxford's notoriously busy bypasses (north, south, east, and west) and its rigid one-way system in the heart of town. I would normally park my car on the market car park, which was a hundred yards from the police station, on the other side of the bypass, but it would be a drive of almost a quarter of a mile through heavy and intransigent traffic. It would take me the better part of twenty minutes to get there by car. I could walk it in less than five.

That timescale reckoned without the intervention of Vic Hillman, who collared me the moment I came out of the station.

"Are you shifting that piece of junk?" He waved an irritable arm in the direction of my car.

"No."

"You'd better. Because if you don't, I'll book you. This car park is for members of the public who have business in this station. You're on your way out, so obviously your business is done with."

"True, but Paddy gave me permission to leave it here for half an hour. Take it up with him, Minx."

I didn't wait for him to say any more, and I certainly wasn't prepared to listen to the swearing.

Three o'clock in the afternoon, and Radio

Haxford were cruising towards the end of the day shift when the security guard let me in.

Olivia greeted me with her usual good humour. "Hello, Mrs Mapper. Unusual seeing you here on a Friday afternoon."

"It's Thursday, love."

"Oh. Course it is." Aside from delivering a new variation on my name, the idiot girl seemed to accept that if it was unusual to turn up on Friday, it was quite normal for me to show my face on Thursday. It wasn't, but her reaction indicated her general level of intelligence. I swear, Cappy the Cat had more brains.

"I need a word with your dad," I said, pointing to Eric's back where he sat at his workstation in front of the broadcast booth. "Can you get him for me?"

"Sure. You want a cup of tea or something while you're here?"

I had never in all the time I'd been working for the station, accepted one of Olivia's cups of tea. Not that she was capable of ruining it, but she was more than capable of coming back with a cup of… something that rhymes with tea. Need I say more?

After Olivia whispered in his ear, Eric took off his headset, left his seat, and joined me by the door. "Something on your mind, Chrissy?"

"The Christine Capper Interview. You asked me the other day if I had any ideas, well, I've just come across one today."

"I'm listening."

Over the next few minutes, I gave him an outline of Tel Wheatley's experiences, and stressed his willingness to be interviewed on radio.

"The only thing is, he wants to speak to you in

advance."

"That shouldn't be a problem. How do you feel about it?"

"I was the one who suggested it. Let's be honest about it, Eric, racism gets a lot of coverage in the press, but that hasn't stamped it out. All it's done is push it underground, made it less visible, less tangible. I'm not suggesting that Tel can't get work because he's black. He's the one saying that, but there were any number of builders in the Engine House and he admitted that most of them were there because they're unemployed and work is scarce. I also realise, it's an issue, rather than any form of entertainment, but I do remember him when he played for Haxford Town and he's a good man. If you can get Jill to work on a series of questions that blends in comparisons to his sporting prowess back then, to his situation right now, and the amount of prejudice he's suffered all his life, we should be able to put together an interesting programme."

"Leave it with me. I'll bell you, and we'll make the necessary arrangements for me and Wheatley to meet."

Happy with the outcome, I moved to Jill Bleaker's desk. She greeted me with a half-smile that was hardly welcoming. "Hiya, Chrissy. Everything all right?"

"Mostly," I said. "I need to know who told you I was joining the Haxford Losers Club."

"Well, I don't really want—"

I cut her off before she could make her excuses. "It was Heidi Flanagan, wasn't it?"

I was surprised how quickly she replied. "Yes. It

was. I know her of old and she was asking me about Haxford (not so) Heavies. I asked why and she told me about the diet shake Georgie Tibbett sells. She also told me Georgie had hired you."

"Well it cost her the ultimate price, didn't it?"

"I know. I read about it in the Recorder."

With that, I left the studio, and even though I was pining for a cuppa at Terry's Tea Bar, I decided against it. Half past three, Paddy had said, and if I didn't move by then, Minx would book me for sure. In fact, judging from the mood he was in, he might very well tow my car away.

A further quarter of an hour or more later, I had filled the petrol tank, and I was parked near the entrance to CutCost, and was making my way up the travelator to the cafeteria, where I enjoyed a cup of tea and risked a scone with jam and cream. Dennis always insisted that such a treat carried about 600 calories, but I was well aware of his capacity for exaggeration. According to me, it was no more than 100 calories, and with the amount of walking I'd done today, I'd probably burned that off already.

The news that Heidi Flanagan had been talking to Jill was not good for Georgie, but I still believed in my client's innocence, even though it was looking more and more doubtful.

While I ate, I took out my smartphone and rang Walton Endicott.

Like Paddy Quinn, he wasn't particularly pleased to hear from me. "I thought I telled thee yesterday, I've nowt to say to thee."

"Hear me out, Mr Endicott. I'm not asking about your wife's sad demise. I've been told that when they were first constructing Haxford Health Spa, you found poisonous plants on the perimeter."

"Monkshood," he said.

"Pardon me?"

"Monkshood. Aconitum napellus if tha wants to get technical. Also known as wolfsbane. Deadly stuff if tha doesn't know what tha's doing wi' it."

"And is it right that you continue to find this stuff today?"

"I've telled that prat, Leeming, until I'm blue in t' bloody face, but he couldn't care less. And he won't until one of his well-off members drops dead."

"That, Mr Endicott, is all I need to know."

"Aye, well, I had the police on earlier. They think that aconite is what killed our lass. Happen they're right but it's nowt to do with me. I won't go anywhere near the stuff unless somebody pays me extra to deal wi' it. Officially, it's a job for the Council, but tha knows what they're like. A waste of space and public money."

That was all the information I needed. I bid him good day, finished my tea and scone, and then began the tiresome, weekly task of getting in our shopping.

Forty-five minutes later, I dropped the bags in the boot, climbed into the car, and took out my mobile once again. This time I rang the spa.

"Could I speak to Mr Leeming, please."

"And who shall I say is calling?"

"Christine Capper, private investigator."

"I doubt very much that he will want to speak to you, Mrs Capper."

Why did these people have to be so obdurate? It was a question I asked myself while I thought up my next rejoinder. "And how will you react when the police come to see him after I speak to them?"

"Hold the line a moment, please."

The line went dead, and *Eye of the Tiger* began to play. It was preferable to Sinatra flying to the moon, but even so, it wasn't exactly my vintage. I couldn't remember who sang it, but I could see the relevance in its relation to one of the Rocky movies and the spa's mission on health and fitness.

A moment later, the music died, and Leeming's voice came over the phone. "Mrs Capper. What can I do for you?"

"I need to speak to you, Mr Leeming. I wondered if it would be convenient for me to come along and see you tomorrow morning."

"In relation to?"

"Poisonous plants growing on the perimeter of your premises, and your refusal to do anything about them."

"I really don't think—"

I cut him off. "It might interest you to know there's a suspicion that one of those plants was used in the murder of Annie Louise Endicott. There's also a suspicion that her murder was indirectly linked to the murder of Heidi Flanagan."

The change was exactly as I expected it. Fast and ingratiating. "Would half-past ten tomorrow morning be suitable?"

"I'll see you then."

Satisfied with my afternoon's work, I luxuriated in the glow for a moment and then with a shock of pure horror, I realised I still had chilled and frozen foods in the boot, and with a sense of urgency, I started the engine, reversed out of the parking space, and made for home. That shopping had been sat in the boot of my hot car for the last twenty minutes. What did that say about me as a housewife? And I'm old-fashioned, so I do mean housewife, not homemaker.

When it came to the case, I had a number of loose threads, and I wasn't sure exactly how they came together, but I was certain that everything would become apparent over the coming days, and as always, that brought an element of satisfaction to me. At the beginning of the year I seriously questioned my abilities as a private investigator, but events since then had proven that I was worthy of the licence. The best, the *only* private detective in Haxford.

Chapter Eighteen

Cappy the Cat didn't look too pleased to see me until he laid eyes on the shopping bags coming in from the car. He knew only too well that such a load signalled food, and that was enough to guarantee his undying loyalty.

After dragging the shopping in, putting away the chilled and frozen items (the tub of soft scoop ice cream had suffered the most, and was now so soft I could probably pour it) I made myself a cup of tea, grabbed a couple of chocolate digestives and my laptop, and made my way into the conservatory. I could have pressed Leeming into seeing me that afternoon, but I needed to check on the seriousness of monkshood's toxicity before challenging him. Endicott declared it dangerous and I didn't know enough about it to argue with him.

I was about to get into it, when the phone rang. Lindsey Sandals from Foulsham Probate & Property.

"Christine Capper, and before you ask, yes it is Christine. I don't employ a secretary."

"It's Lindsey from Foulsham's, Mrs Capper. I wondered if you'd sent those documents yet?"

"I was just about to send them to you, Lindsey," I lied. In fact, I'd forgotten them until she mentioned them. Multitasking; it played havoc with my memory sometimes. "I've had a hectic day and I've only just got in."

"I suppose life must be quite busy for radio presenters."

"Not for me," I argued. "I only do a couple of hours a week. In fact, it's my work as a private eye that's kept me to-ing and fro-ing these last couple of days."

"Ah, now, I'm glad you mentioned that because it's part of the reason I'm ringing."

This was new. Up to press she and I had got on like the Prime Minister and Leader of the Opposition during PMQs (that's Prime Minister's Questions for those who don't know).

Mrs open-toed footwear went on. "Are you a licenced PI? I appreciate that there's no requirement in UK law for such qualifications, but—"

"I used to be a police officer," I interrupted, "and when I decided to turn private, I went through the training and yes, I am licenced and answerable to a regulatory organisation. Obviously, if I did something wrong, they could withdraw my licence, but it wouldn't necessarily stop me from working in the industry. What precisely do you want, Lindsey?"

"One of the investigators we use in your part of the world has just been prosecuted and jailed for threatening behaviour while working on a repossession case."

"Well, it wouldn't happen with me because I don't do bad debts or repo work. I'm quite choosy about the cases I take on. Usually matrimonial or people tracing. I don't do confrontation." It sounded odd telling her that. During my current case I'd had nothing but confrontation, even with my client.

Her voice carried a smile. "That's exactly what we like to hear. Tell me, would you like to be added to our lists for interviewing potential heirs after we've traced them, or even tracing them when we can't find them?"

A vision of Dennis sprang to mind, and prompted me to ask, "How much does it pay?"

"Your rates, but we would expect you to be, er, reasonable."

"In that case, I charge sixty pounds and out of pocket expenses. Those would mainly be petrol, so in the Haxford area, not much, but further afield, it's more expensive. How does that sound?"

"Are your charges negotiable?"

"Within reason. Why? Do they sound too expensive?"

"We usually pay about fifty an hour, and we insist on an itemised bill."

"No problem. I could go with that." Especially, I thought to myself, when I had people like Kim Aspinall who would help me for free. "Where do we go from here?"

"We need to see your licence, we need to contact the organisation you're registered with, and we need two independent references."

"How about a serving police officer, and senior producer/director at Radio Haxford?"

"Sounds ideal."

"Give me twenty-four hours to get the licence scanned and uploaded, and I'll get them to you."

"The moment we've cleared everything, we'll get back to you with a standard agreement."

I ended the call with a glow of satisfaction as all-consuming as… toasted teacakes in Terry's Tea Bar. (You thought I was going to say something a good deal more passionate, didn't you? And that just goes to show you how passionate I am about Terry's toasted teacakes.)

I did not, for one moment, imagine there would be a flood of work coming in from them. I mean, how many missing heirs could there be in the Haxford area? But any work which tested my investigative skills (poking my nose in, as Dennis would say) was more than welcome, and think of the vlogging opportunities.

To celebrate, I treated myself to another chocolate digestive and then went back to the job I first thought of, researching monkshood/wolfsbane/*aconitum napellus*, call it what you will.

It soon became apparent that Walt Endicott had slightly overstated the situation. It was a pretty little plant, which grew on tallish stems, with a dark blue to purple flowers, and its toxicity was well documented. It was lethal to human beings and most animals alike, and yet there were any number of people who liked and planted them in their private gardens. The one thing stressed in the article I read was that when handling monkshood stout gloves were an absolute necessity. It appeared that aconite, the toxin concerned, could be absorbed through the skin, and again, even in small amounts, it would make the victim quite ill. It could also kill if the handler absorbed too much of it on his/her hands.

This opened up a whole new possibility, one which the police had perhaps already considered, but knowing Paddy Quinn's hastiness, it was entirely possible that they'd missed it.

Right away, I rang Mandy. She answered, but it was obvious she was not in the best frame of mind.

"Paddy's taken over, and he's ordered me to shut my trap, especially when speaking to you."

"And of course, you're going to obey his command?"

"What do you want, Chrissy?"

I explained how I'd spoken to Paddy earlier in the day, and he'd mentioned aconite. "Did you get the toxicology results back? What's more, did you get the results back from the search of Georgie Tibbett's garage, and the analysis of the diet shakes?"

"Yes, yes, and yes. Happy now?"

"I will be when you tell me whether you found any traces of aconite in the shakes or the garage."

"No. We didn't. Well, not yet. We're still on with the garage. What's on your mind, Chrissy?"

"I've just been doing a bit of my own research, and I'm sure you're aware that aconite can be absorbed through the skin."

"Yes. We knew about it. But before you ask, it was too late to check on the glass that Annie used to drink the last shake. It had been washed, thoroughly cleaned. When we asked Endicott about it, he said Annie must have done it because he didn't touch anything when he got home and found her. I haven't had a detailed look at the PM report, but I'm sure that somewhere it says she ingested the poison. I read that to mean she swallowed it."

"So if it was in the shake, and not, for example, a cup of tea, it meant someone tampered with that shake and dropped the aconite in it."

"Bang on. But as houseproud as she was, the wrapper had already been disposed of, and our guys found as many as half a dozen of them in the dustbin. They ignored them, and true to form, the bins were emptied yesterday. By the time we got this information this morning, it was too late. That wrapper, along with all the others has gone to the council incinerator."

I remained silent for a moment, wondering what to ask next, but I never got the chance to ask anything as Mandy went on.

"Right now, we're not looking at Georgie in respect of Annie's murder. We still think she did it, but it'll be a tough one to prove. Instead, we're looking at Heidi Flanagan's death. It was murder, it was blunt force trauma, and we still figure it was Georgie."

"Not much more I can say then, is there? I can tell you I've an appointment with Fletcher Leeming tomorrow morning. I'll level with you, Mandy. There are other suspects, including Jonathan Ambrose, Patricia Keenan, and Tel Wheatley, but the front runner is Ambrose."

"Why?"

"Heidi hit on him, he said no – according to him – but Heidi says different. Whatever the truth, she was very complimentary about him, and I've had similar opinions from other quarters, namely Sandra Limpkin."

Mandy clucked. "Sandra's not the choosiest woman in Haxford, is she?"

"My point precisely. She doesn't normally

complain about the men she's entertained. Having said that, I can't find anything to link him to Annie Endicott. Anyway, I'll give you a bell tomorrow, after I've spoken to Leeming."

"Do that. Paddy's getting on my nerves right now. This is one of the toughest we've ever come across, Chrissy, and I don't care what he says. We need some help."

"Consider it done."

I ended the call and sank into my glum thoughts. The best detective in Haxford? I thought so, but I still couldn't work out how everything tied together. It was all very well blaming Jonathan Ambrose, but I had absolutely nothing to tie him to either crime. I didn't like him, but I had enough experience to ensure that did not lead me along the much beaten path of assuming guilt.

Indeed, when I stopped to think about it, the clearest suspect in Annie Endicott's killing was her husband. He knew about the plants, he and Annie did not enjoy the friendliest of marriages. After him, I would have to side with Mandy and line up against Georgie Tibbett.

The killing of Heidi Flanagan was an altogether more frustrating issue. I knew nothing about her other than the scuttlebutt I'd picked up and as matters stood, I had absolutely nothing to link her death to Annie's. In plain English, I (and the police) could be looking for two killers.

I'd always found that the best way to solve a problem was to distract yourself from it for a while, so I took out one of the rolls of wallpaper and held it up against the wall between the side door and the conservatory door.

Cappy the Cat popped his head in to see if there was any chance of food, and gave me a sort of scathing look which said, 'She's at it again. Why does everything in this house come before me?' Then he disappeared back into the conservatory and out through the back door. He would take it out on Barbara Timmins's lawn.

The wallpaper looked absolutely perfect. Along with the other redecoration, it would give the kitchen a bright, sparkling new look, almost as if it was ready to be the 'after' vision in one of those TV adverts where the actors take a mop, run it once over the floor with an expensive cleaner, and the whole place shines like a new installation.

That was fine on an open wall such as that between the two doors, but how would it look above the cooker?

I crossed the kitchen again, reached over the hob and held it up above the tiles. Heaven. That was my assessment. It was comforting to know that my skills of choice had not diminished.

The job done, satisfied with the results, I made a fresh cup of tea, returned to the conservatory, and within a matter of moments, the problem of the two murders obsessed me again.

I'd come across some tough cases in the past, but none as lacking in evidence as this one, and I was still mulling the problem, still making no progress when Dennis got home just before seven.

He was in as mean a mood as I'd seen him for quite some time. Every query, every comment was greeted with a surly grunt. We passed our evening meal in near silence, he concentrating on the classifieds in the Haxford Recorder, me trying to think of some way of breaching his tetchy mood.

By eight o'clock, I'd had enough, and decided that tact, encouragement, was not the way forward.

"Dennis, will you please say exactly what's on your mind."

"Nowt."

"When I ask you to be honest, that's what I expect. Not more sulks. Now what is it?"

He closed the newspaper. "All right. If you wanna know, it's money."

I had an idea where he was going, but I played my dumb act. "Money? We're all right for money."

"Happen we are, but the way you're spending it, we won't be for much longer. I meanersay, letting Snoddy take you apart like that. Four hundred notes for a dab of paint and a bit of wallpaper?"

"I didn't think it was too bad. And I've added to it since."

He gaped. "What?"

"The wallpaper cost me sixty pounds."

"Sixty blinking quid? Why didn't you ring me? I could have had a word—"

"I'm the one that does all the work in this kitchen, Dennis. You're hopeless in here. You don't even know which liquid to put in the dishwasher. You've admitted it no end of times. Well, I want the place sprucing up. And it won't stop there. I want the living room done before Christmas."

"I don't know if I'll have time," he protested.

"This entire house needs doing from top to bottom." It sounded a bizarre statement considering it was a bungalow and therefore all on one level. "I can't remember the last time we decorated and the place is looking shabby."

"Yes, but I said, I'm allus working."

"In that case, you'd better work out how much overtime you need to put in to pay for someone like Barry Snodgrass to do it. Now shut up and deal with it."

Chapter Nineteen

I had no choice but to be up early on Friday morning. Barry was due at half past eight and I had to be at Haxford Health Spa for half past ten.

Dennis was not in a communicative mood. When I told him I probably wouldn't be able to use the cooker because the tiling cement behind it would need time to set, as a result of which he'd be getting a microwaved TV dinner for his evening meal, all he said was, "It'll have to do I suppose."

Once he left for work, I jumped in the shower. I had plenty of time, so I suppose I could have waited, but I wasn't too keen on showering and dressing when I was alone with a strange man in the house. By strange, I mean that Barry was a stranger to me. On the other hand, even if he was some kind of sex pest, I'd be in a tricky position. No use expecting Cappy the Cat to protect me. All anyone had to do was put him a feed down and nothing in the world would matter but the food. I could become the victim of a serial rapist and he wouldn't give it a passing thought.

By eight o'clock, I was back in the bedroom, considering my attire. Under normal circumstances, when meeting executive types like Fletcher Leeming, it would be formal business wear: dark skirt, white blouse, dark jacket, court shoes, but I remembered he was dressed in a shell suit, a throwback to the late 80s and early 90s. I wouldn't be seen dead in a shell suit these days, and I didn't want to appear as if I was applying for membership of the spa. Eventually, I decided on a pair of dark blue denims, and with Val's warning of his leering habit, a plain, white T-shirt which fitted snugly round my neck. I finished the ensemble with my trusty, black trainers. I wasn't sure whether he was as pompous as he sounded on Tuesday evening, but if so, my casual approach should help to disrupt him.

Barry Snodgrass was about five minutes late when he eventually reversed his van into our drive and parked next to my car.

"Rotten traffic," he said as he carried a bucket of tile cement, grout, and several packs of tiles into the kitchen.

"No problem, Barry. Sit yourself down and I'll make you some tea." I brewed two beakers, put the sugar bowl on the table for him, clicked a few sweeteners into mine, then sat opposite. "What's your master plan for the day?"

Dropping two spoonfuls of sugar into his tea, stirring vigorously, he nodded towards the cooker. "I'll drag your stove out, chip the old tiles off, and put the new ones on. After that, I'll get on with the ceiling. I've got dust sheets in the van, but you might have the odd splashes here and there. It's no big deal, Christine. It's only emulsion, so it will clean off easily enough. Then tomorrow, I'll get on with the prep and papering. All things being equal, I should be done by late tomorrow afternoon. If not, I'll have to come back again on Sunday morning."

"It all sounds fine. The only thing is, Barry, I'm in the middle of a complex case, and I have to go out this morning. I'll leave you and teabags and milk so you can make a brew whenever you want, but if you'd prefer, I'll leave Cappy the Cat with Mrs McQuarrie next door. He won't pester you too much, and I can leave both conservatory doors open so he can come and go out as he pleases. I should be back by about lunchtime, but I might have to go out again this afternoon."

"It's no problem, lass. Is he friendly, your cat?"

"When you're feeding him, yes. At any other time, he considers people to be his mortal enemy. The only thing I'm bothered about, is him walking over your dust sheets while you're painting the ceiling, and him getting splashed in paint."

He laughed. "You can always give him a bath."

I shook my head. "Not advisable. Not if you like your eyes where they're supposed to be rather than clawed out." I reached a decision. "I'll take him to Mrs McQuarrie. She's used to him."

"As you wish." He drank his tea and stood up. "I'd better get on with it."

With his usual skill at arms, Cappy the Cat had disappeared, presumably paying his customary calls on Barbara Timmins and wherever else he wandered, but it gave me the opportunity to arrange with Hazel McQuarrie to leave him.

As usual, she was only too pleased to help. "Bring him round when you're ready, Christine. I'll keep an eye on him."

"He'll be there in a few minutes, and I should be

back by twelve or just after."

"No rush. Just get him here."

It would not be Cappy the Cat's best option. He hated being left with Hazel. When he was with her he had to do as he was told and not as he pleased. As a consequence, when he came back in and laid eyes on the pet carrier, he turned to run for it, but I got to both doors before him, and trapped him in the kitchen. I had the usual fight to get him in the pet carrier, but with the time coming up to half past nine, I carried him round to Hazel's, along with his dish, and some food, and promised to pick him up when I got back. The last I saw, he was staring at me from the confines of the pet carrier, an evil glare that promised nuclear retaliation the next time he saw me.

When I got back, Barry had the cooker pulled out, and was working at the back, gently prising the old tiles away from the wall and tossing them into an open space where they broke into large and small pieces. I was tempted to get out the brush and dustpan, but I didn't have time.

"I'm on my way, Barry. I'll leave you with it, and I should be back by noon."

"No worries."

All in all, I was relieved to climb behind the wheel of the car, start the engine, let the windows down, and pull out of the drive.

For the third day in succession there was not a cloud to be seen in the sky, and I felt relaxed, comfortable during the drive to the spa. Behind that calm, however, was a raging storm of indecision, questions to be asked, and a determination to get some answers rather than evasion.

I arrived at the spa about ten minutes ahead of our meeting, and after a brief exchange with the young woman on reception, I waited for Leeming to appear.

I expected him in a shell suit, or maybe further back, turning out in a pair of bell bottomed jeans. No such luck. When he finally arrived in reception, he was wearing a dark blue business suit, white shirt, and company tie snuggled up to his Adam's apple.

"Mrs Capper. A pleasure to see you again." He offered his hand and I shook it. A pleasure? I wondered idly whether he would be of the same opinion once I'd done speaking to him. "Shall we repair to my office?"

Repair? That was a new one for Haxford. Normally, it would be, 'come on, lass, let's get down to it'.

His office was in the administration area, opposite the cafeteria. Small, comfortable, uncluttered, he dropped into an executive chair and waved me to the seat opposite.

"Beautiful weather," he announced. "Much preferable to the rain of the last few weeks."

I recognised the jingle of conversational small change, and replied in kind, accepted his offer of a cup of tea, and then, once it was delivered, got down to business.

"Two murders, Mr Leeming, both victims connected with a slimming group operating on your premises. It doesn't look too good for Haxford Health Spa, and I've no wish to appear critical of your operation, but there are a lot of questions to be asked, particularly concerning the victims, Annie Louise Endicott and Heidi Flanagan, and beyond them, Georgie Tibbett, Karen Dawkins, and Jonathan Ambrose. All I need to know is whether you can throw any light on disputes involving these people."

He drummed his fingers on the desk, took a sip of tea, and put the cup down. It seemed important to him that it sat precisely in the centre of the saucer, and I diagnosed a man carefully constructing his response.

"One does not like to cast aspersions, madam, but over the course of the last year or so, I've had a series of complaints about Mrs Tibbett. Mostly, they concerned her attitude, her approach to people. She was very outspoken. Nothing wrong with that, of course, but she seemed incapable of treating people, her members in particular, with any degree of diplomacy."

"May I ask who the complaints came from? Anyone in particular?"

"Ms Dawkins, primarily, a few from Jonathan Ambrose. I'm not given to gossip, but I understand that there was some kind of relationship between Mrs Tibbett and Ambrose before he settled down with Ms Dawkins. When speaking to Mrs Tibbett, I stressed that such matters were of no concern to us, but they should be dealt with in private, not in public."

"And her response?"

"Quite, er, brutal, and using a good deal of, er, industrial language, if you take my meaning."

I nodded. "I used to be a police officer. I'm quite used to it. Did Mrs Endicott or Mrs Flanagan have any occasion to complain about Georgie?"

"Not directly. But members of my staff reported both women as being equally candid as Mrs Tibbett. Frankly, Mrs Capper, I regret the day I ever allowed the Haxford Losers Club to use our facilities."

That was a puzzle. "According to information I received, you approached Georgie Tibbett."

He shook his said. "Not so. In fact, she approached me. I told her that we already had one diet group working in the centre, Haxford (not so) Heavies, and she persuaded me that healthy competition was good for not only the diet groups but the centre also. I allowed myself to be persuaded. It was a bad decision on my part."

I cast my mind back to the last time I had met this man. "Tuesday night, you called into the diet club shortly after the police had taken Georgie away. You said you were looking for her because you always collected her rent, or whatever you want to call it, in the middle of her class. I find that odd. In that kind of business arrangement, such payments would usually be made by direct debit or electronic transfer. It would be very unusual for her to make payments in cash."

"Curiously enough, that is not so. True, there are many tutors and organisers who pay by direct debit, but equally, there are those who don't make vast amounts of money from their efforts and pay us by cash. Mrs Tibbett was one such. However, you are correct about my visit to her class on Tuesday evening. She had already paid the room rental. In fact, I'd had another complaint about her, this time from Ambrose, and I needed a serious word with her. Frankly, Mrs Capper, I was considering terminating her use of the spa. Naturally, I didn't know she'd been arrested. Not until you told me, although I must admit I was aware of a police presence."

His confession, and the information he'd given me cast doubts in my mind. Many people, Georgie Tibbett amongst them, had been lying to me.

I was tempted to ask him about the exchange between him and Heidi Flanagan outside the Barley Mow but I needed time to think about things, so I drew his attention away from the relevant personalities, and asked, "Let's talk about the presence of monkshood on the perimeter of your grounds."

He was quite blasé about it. "The keywords, Mrs Capper, are 'on the perimeter'. When Endicott first brought them to my attention, I went over there to see exactly what he was talking about, and these plants are growing wild, but they are beyond the boundary of our grounds. Endicott himself admitted that technically, it was a job for the local authority, and I duly contacted them. They said they'd deal with the matter, and the next time I went over there, they'd put up a warning sign, advising people that the particular plants are hazardous to health."

I tutted. That was entirely typical of Haxford Borough Council. "I don't know about hazardous to health," I said. "According to my reading, they're lethal. The poison can even be absorbed through the skin. Could you tell me where they are, and would you mind if I strolled over and had a look at them?"

"No, of course not. Better than that, I'll show you."

He left his desk, crossed the office, kicked off his shoes and pulled on a pair of wellington boots. "The last time I was over there, it was quite muddy," he explained, and he made me wish I'd brought a pair of wellies with me.

We left the building and emerged into bright sunshine, but far away to my right, I could see clouds building up. A light breeze came from the west and I guessed that the three-day heatwave would be coming to an end, if not today, then certainly tomorrow.

We walked away in the opposite direction, towards Wakey Moor Woods. It was no more than a small copse, and really didn't deserve the title 'woods' but I knew it to be overgrown and difficult to negotiate. And no, I'm not speaking from personal experience, but a few friends had wandered in there with their boyfriends. I don't know what they were doing. Probably picking bluebells. (If that sounds naive, the real truth is, I didn't want to know what they were doing but I could make an educated guess and it had little to do with picking bluebells.)

Leeming led the way across the carefully cultivated grasses belonging to the spa, and across a short space where the rougher moorland growth, still soggy underfoot, began to take over. On the very edge of the woods, was the sign he had talked about, cautioning passers-by that the plants, *aconitum napellus*, was indeed toxic, hazardous to health. However, there were no plants to be seen.

"I can't understand what's happened to them," Leeming said. "I'm certain that the council people never bothered to dig them out and take them away."

"As far as my research goes, they're not exactly common," I said, "but they do grow wild, especially in soil that retains moisture, and let's face it, these moors are known for their damp environment, aren't they? And they're grown in gardens all over the country, all over the world."

Leeming nodded sagely. "That doesn't explain where these have gone, though does it."

"Oh, I know where they've gone, Mr Leeming. I just don't know who took them." He laid a kind of shocked stare on me. "Annie Endicott drank them."

Chapter Twenty

The interlude with Leeming proved more informative than I could ever have hoped. I knew now where the poison came from, although it didn't take a genius to work that out. I had more than an inkling from the moment Endicott told me. I also knew just how much people had not been telling me, and how some – Georgie Tibbett and Jonathan Ambrose in particular – had been lying. Well, I say lying, what I really mean is Georgie had painted herself in a more generous light than was really the case. And in the case of Ambrose, he never told me he'd laid complaints about Georgie to the spa management.

It all added up to one of two things. Either Georgie Tibbett murdered Annie Endicott, or someone else (Ambrose?) did the deed in an attempt to point the finger at Georgie and get her out of his/her hair. And it was a safe bet that whoever killed Annie also dealt with Heidi. No prizes for guessing which solution I preferred.

The dashboard clock read a few minutes past eleven. I promised Hazel McQuarrie I'd be back to collect Cappy the Cat by noon. Did I have time to pay Georgie Tibbett a visit?

No contest. Hazel would understand.

Ten minutes later, I pulled up outside Georgie's place, marched to the door and rang the bell. No answer. I hammered on the door. No answer. I began to worry. The last time I spoke to her, she was seriously depressed. Had she decided to take the same way out as Annie Endicott, but of her own accord rather than at the hands of a murderer?

I looked through the windows, I couldn't see anything or anyone. Time to take action.

I took out my phone, and rang Mandy's direct number. "I think something might have happened to Georgie," I said. "I'm outside her house and I can't get an answer."

"Hardly surprising. Paddy's held her overnight. She's in the cells here."

Why didn't I think of that first? Hadn't I warned her that they might keep her? "Is there any chance I could speak to her, Mandy?"

"Yes. Two chances. Slim, and so remote that no sensible bookie would give you a price."

I tutted. "I've come across more information this morning, and I really need to speak to her, Mands. I mean, you can be there with me if you want. All I need is five minutes of her time – and yours."

"Paddy's out and about doing what Paddy does best. Making a nuisance of himself. Why don't you come along now, tell me what it is you know, and then we'll see about letting you talk to Georgie."

"I'll be there in twenty minutes." Ending that call, I rang Hazel and explained that I might be a tad late getting home.

"It's no problem, Chrissy. You take your time, love. Cappy the Cat seems perfectly content sleeping on my settee."

Some chance, I thought as I rang off. Knowing that little rebel, he was probably plotting his next campaign of anti-human terrorism.

I started the engine, turned the car round in less than four shunts, and sped off towards Haxford.

Fifteen angst-ridden minutes later, I parked on the market, locked up, and hurried across to the police station. For once, it was Rehana Suleman rather than Vic Hillman on reception, so instead of earache, she let me go straight through to Mandy's office.

Haxford's CID's finest (until the day dawned when my son would claim the mantle) greeted me brightly. "Here she is, Prissy Chrissy Porridge, Hercule's great-great-great-look-alike." She glanced down at the blood red carpet. "Thanks, Chrissy. Just what we needed on a Friday morning. You dragging a load of mud into my office."

I glanced down at the footprints. "Oops. Sorry, Mandy. I've been scouring Wakey Moor Woods and they're still damp after last week's rain."

"I don't want to know about you sneaking into the woods with some toyboy when Dennis isn't looking, but I'll make sure the cleaners know you're to blame. Park your BTM, I'll order some tea, and you can bring me up to speed." She reached for the telephone.

"Paddy's still not here?"

"Haven't a clue, couldn't care less. It's Mandy Hiscoe," she said into the receiver. "Two teas, my office, ten minutes ago, please." She dropped the phone. "Okay, Chrissy. The floor's yours."

Over the next few minutes, I gave her a blow by blow account of my meeting with Fletcher Leeming, and our brief visit to the edge of the woods.

"To be fair, Chrissy, we would have got round to checking those woods, especially after you told us what Endicott had said. But it still doesn't tell us who took the monkshood, my money's still on Georgie Tibbett."

"I'm hedging my bets," I admitted. "She's not been telling me the whole truth and nothing but the truth. She's exaggerated certain aspects and I need to confront her about that. If she's covering up her unpopularity, what else might she be hiding? The same goes for Ambrose. According to Leeming, he made more than his fair share of complaints about Georgie."

We were interrupted by a uniformed constable delivering two beakers of canteen tea. When he'd gone, Mandy picked up the phone again and began to punch in the numbers. "I'll try to get a quick word with Paddy. Trouble is, Chrissy, if I go behind his back, you know what'll happen."

"He'll kick you through the roof, and bill you for new slates."

She smiled and held up a hand for silence. "Paddy? Mandy. I've got Christine with me, and we really need her to talk to Georgie."

I couldn't hear what was being said, but I could detect Paddy's voice rattling fifteen to the dozen. It wasn't difficult to work out what he was saying, and I guessed most of it would be about me and it would not be particularly complimentary.

"I know that, but she's not trying to get Georgie off the hook," Mandy persisted. "In fact, if it goes the way I think it will, she might actually close the case."

Another rattled squawking came from the receiver, and I could see Mandy's annoyance beginning to rise.

"Has anyone ever told you what a total prat you are?"

Once again, I couldn't hear Paddy's response, but I guessed that this time it would be a warning to Mandy concerning insubordination.

"If you don't want me slinging insults at you, you should use your head. It's our job to seal the deal on this case, and as far as I'm concerned it doesn't matter how we get to it. If necessary, Paddy, I'll go over your head."

More waffle came from the other end, but Mandy finally brought the call to an end.

"Don't worry. I'll make sure everything's above board." She slammed the receiver down, took a healthy swallow of tea, and then smiled at me. "He's agreed, but let's just say he might cross you off his Christmas card list."

I smiled back. "And I'll be heartbroken about that. Shall we get to it?"

Less than ten minutes later, we were in an interview room facing Georgie. Irma Orson was also there, a means of ensuring that there were two police officers as well as me.

Mandy got the ball rolling. "Chrissy has some questions for you, Georgie. This interview is not official. I won't be recording it, and you don't have to answer any of Chrissy's questions, but bear in mind, if you don't, I will then call your solicitor, and we'll go to a formal interview, during which I will put the same questions to you. Do you understand?"

She nodded. "I'm not stupid." Her attention swung to me. "What do you want to know?"

Two days ago, I felt sorry for this woman. Now I was just angry, and annoying Christine Capper was never a wise move, as Dennis would testify.

"A couple of days ago we spoke at length in your house, and you told me a series of – let's say untruths. It's more polite than lies."

"You offered to help, and I told you the absolute truth."

"You're doing it again. I spoke to Fletcher Leeming this morning, and he brought me up to speed. He never approached you to set up Haxford Losers Club at the spa. It was the other way round. You asked him."

"I didn't."

"You're telling me he's lying? He doesn't have the gumption to lie. If I'm to help you, Georgie, I need the absolute God's honest truth from you. Did you ask Fletcher Leeming to setup your diet club at the spa?"

She was silent for a good minute. In the end, she nodded, and then turned on the appeal. "Don't you think I was in enough trouble as it was? Arrested for something I didn't do, my business on the verge of collapse? All I was doing was trying to smooth out the rough edges."

Partially satisfied, I pressed home the attack. "Why did you want to be at the spa? Why did you want your club meetings on the same night as Karen's?"

Another silence followed. "You don't know all the ins and outs of it because I didn't tell you.

Moving there had nothing to do with Karen... Well, it did, but not directly. It was more to do with Ambrose."

Mandy spoke this time. "What about him?"

"I told Christine the other day that I had an affair with Ambrose. I was guilty, it wrecked my marriage, and when that happened, he set his sights on my sister." The fire began to burn in her eyes again. "What I didn't tell you was that he was always borrowing money from me. I didn't mind. I was getting my jollies, but when Brian left me, I was down on my uppers. Not as bad as I am now, obviously, but I was on the way to the gutter. He never paid me any of the money back. It was only a few hundred quid, but I could have done with it. When he hitched on to Karen, I knew he would do the same to her. That's why I moved to the spa. Not that Karen would listen to me."

I recalled my brief conversation with Sandra Limpkin, and the way she'd told me that Ambrose was only interested in two things: the obvious and taking as much money from the women as he could.

I didn't bother taking any notes because Mandy was scribbling away on an A4 pad. Instead I switched tack.

"Leeming also told me that he had any number of complaints about you, mostly from Karen, a few from Ambrose. They concerned your general attitude to them and to people in general."

"Same thing. I tried to tell Karen what was going on or what would be going on before long and she told me to go forth and multiply. You understand what I mean? I persisted. I wasn't about to see my sister fleeced by a man like Ambrose. So she complained to Leeming – about me, not Ambrose, and he took it up with me. I gave him the same answer as Karen gave me. She kept complaining, I tackled Ambrose, and he threw his hat in the ring by complaining to Leeming too. Sure, Heidi Flanagan moaned about me, so did Annie Endicott, but they were complaining that the diet wasn't working, and as far as I understand it, Leeming said it wasn't his problem. He told them to take it up with me. Hell, you were there on Tuesday night. You saw the way Heidi had a go at me. Trust me, it was the same every week. And yet, people like Tel Wheatley, Patricia Keenan, they never complained because they did the job right. They used the shake as a meal replacement. Heidi and Annie used it as a supplement and that's why they weren't losing any weight. You see?"

It all made perfect sense me, but it still did nothing to exonerate Georgie.

"You've been running your group at the spa for about a year. Ever had the occasion to wander over to Wakey Moor Woods?"

She laughed. "Yeah, when I was getting it on with Ambrose. Why?"

I shook my head. "No reason." It would have been simple enough to tell her but I didn't know whether the police had informed her of Annie's poisoning by aconite. "Ever visited Heidi at home?"

She pointed an accusing finger at Mandy. "I've already been through that with the police. No, I never visited her home. Come to that, I don't even know where she lives."

I sat back. "All right, Georgie, that's all I need to

know. Mandy?"

"I can't ask any more questions without Mrs Tibbett's solicitor being present. I can't release you, Georgie. Only Paddy can do that. So I'll ask Irma to take you back to the cells. Thanks for your help." She waited until Georgie had been led away and we were alone again. "So where did that get us, Chrissy?"

I shrugged. "Somewhere, nowhere. It doesn't prove anything one way or the other." I fiddled with my wedding and engagement rings. "I still don't believe it's her. If she's telling the truth, her major concern all along has been her sister. I mean, on the surface, it sounds as if they're constantly at war, but I don't believe that. Remember, Karen actually hired me to help prove Georgie's innocence. I think they're a good deal closer than we think."

"Hmm, maybe so, but that's assuming Georgie's telling the truth. She fed you a line of porkies the other day, what's to say she's not doing the same right now?"

"She admitted that Leeming told it like it was."

"Yes, but we have only her word for it that she moved in order to try and help Karen. For all we know, she could have moved in order to stir up trouble."

I got to my feet. "One way to find out. I'll have a word with Karen. Oh, I don't suppose you know where she lives, do you?"

"I have an address for her, yes. I thought you'd spoken to her once?"

"That was at the spa, and she had Ambrose in tow. Tell you what, it doesn't matter, I'll give her a ring and arrange to see her alone."

And from there, I came out of the police station and rang Karen.

"Mrs Capper. What can I do for you?"

"Any chance I could speak to you, Karen? Preferably alone."

"That depends."

I tutted. "Can I remind you that you hired me to prove Georgie's innocence? I'm close but I really need to speak to you alone."

"Awkward. I'm in town right now."

"Town as in Haxford?"

"Where else?"

"Great. So am I. Do you know Terry's Tea Bar in the market hall?"

"Yep."

"I'll see you there in, what? Ten minutes?"

Chapter Twenty-One

I swear that Terry's Tea Bar was in my debt. The place had no bigger advocate in Haxford than me. I praised their teacakes and their tea at every opportunity.

They did not, however, tempt Karen Dawkins. When I joined her, she already had a cup of tea, and there was no small plate to hint that she'd eaten anything.

"I'm a health freak," she said when I posed the question. "It's rare that I eat in cafés. All right, so I'm overweight, but I am working on it. Frankly, that has more to do with alcohol than food. Now, what did you want?"

"The honest answers to a few questions. I was allowed to see Georgie half an hour ago, and I put the same questions to her. She's given me answers which conflict with earlier ones, and if you expect me to help her, Karen, I'm gonna need you to be absolutely truthful."

She shrugged. "I'll do my best."

"Both Georgie and Jonathan Ambrose led me to believe that Fletcher Leeming had approached her to hold her meetings at the spa. Leeming told me it was the other way round, and Georgie has just confirmed it."

"Chances are that Jonathan heard the story from Georgie herself. Or should I say overheard? But it's true. Georgie approached Fletcher, and she did it out of pure spite. To cause as much grief to me as she possibly could." She shrugged again. "Not that it matters. When all's said and done, she's my sister. I can't stand by and see her accused of a crime I'm sure she didn't commit."

"A commendable attitude, but Georgie says she came to the spa to ensure that Ambrose wasn't trying to milk you for money."

This time she nodded. "Yeah, yeah. Heard it all before. And I know that he borrowed from Georgie when they were, er, seeing each other. She says he never paid her back, he says he did." She leaned forward to ensure I got the next message. "She's paranoid. She's been like that ever since Brian packed his bags and left, but again let's tell it like it is. She was the one who had the affair. What was Brian's supposed to do? Ride with it? Well, he tried, but he couldn't cut it, so he packed his bags and went. After it happened, Georgie would blame anyone for it, including Jonathan, but the truth is, it was all her doing. From there, she went down the pan. Financial problems were at the root of her decline, but instead of laying the blame where it belongs, her affair with Jonathan which caused Brian to walk out, she's laid it off on as many different people she could. She's persuaded herself that everyone is out to get her."

"So eventually, you made complaints against her with Leeming."

"I had to. I tried talking sense into her, but it was like talking to that cup." She aimed a finger at my tea.

"Just so I'm clear on one point, are you saying that Ambrose has never borrowed from you?"

"He borrows now and then, yes. Especially when it's the middle of the month and he's getting short of money. What relationship doesn't have a similar arrangement? I mean, don't you borrow from your husband?" I shook my head. "Different set up. Dennis is self-employed, so am I and we both have a steady stream of income."

"Then you're lucky. For us ordinary mortals, it's a case of waiting for payday to come round. That doesn't apply to me, of course, because like you, I'm self-employed."

"Does Ambrose pay you back?"

She scowled. "That's nothing to do with you."

I took that as a 'no' and came at her from a different angle. "Did he have any entanglement with Heidi Flanagan?"

"What is this, are you trying to clear my sister by pinning it on my partner?"

"There are any number of suspects, Karen, and I'm sorry but yes, Jonathan is one of them. So, I have to say, is Georgie, and so is Walt Endicott. The problem is the two deaths are notably dissimilar. Annie poisoned, Heidi beaten to death."

"You're saying there might be two killers?"

"It's possible but if there's only one, we need to find a motive that's common to both crimes." I switched the conversational track yet again. "Tell me, how well did you know Heidi?"

"Not well. I'd had one or two conversations with her, sure, but that's about it."

"Tuesday evening in the Barley Mow, she was talking to Ambrose when you joined them."

"Yes. She'd just quit the Losers Club and she was asking about the possibility of joining Haxford (not so) Heavies. I didn't like taking people from Georgie's club. To tell the truth, I didn't like the fact that my sister and I were in competition but that was Georgie's decision not mine. I'd rather she stayed with me running Haxford (not so) Heavies, but after Jonathan and I became an item, she couldn't handle it."

"It would have been an uneasy truce, though, wouldn't it?"

"It was already an uneasy truce. It still is. Remember, she bakes the biscuits I sell… Well, she did. The police have closed down her garage while their forensic people go through it."

"You know what they're looking for?"

"Toxins of some description. They won't find anything."

"If they do it'll be bad news for Georgie."

"Listen to me, Christine, it wasn't Georgie. She has some mental health issues. That might sound dramatic, but I think the stress and depression brought on by her divorce and the fallout from it, have affected her judgement, but when it comes to the science, she knows what she's doing."

I racked my mind to see what other questions I might ask, and another potentially sore point occurred. "I don't want to pry, Karen, but when you and Jonathan first got together, did you ever wander over to Wakey Moor Woods?"

She laughed. "What? You think we were like two

teenagers sneaking off for a quickie? I haven't been in Wakey Moor Woods since I was about sixteen. We went back to my place or his now and again."

"So he had his own house?" It was a stupid question. Where did I think he lived when he got involved with Georgie?

"Council flat on Sheffield Road Estate. He still rents it, but he spends most of his time at my place these days and it's only a matter of time before we make it permanent."

This was news. I was under the impression that it was already permanent.

"It's not far from Endicott and his missus as it happens," Karen went on. "In fact, don't quote me on this, but it was Jonathan who helped Endicott secure his contract with the spa. He gave old Wally a good reference."

I found that piece of information more than interesting, but I wasn't about to bring it up with Karen. She'd only leap to Ambrose's defence.

Instead, I finished my tea and said, "I think that's all for now, so I'll leave you to it."

"You still believe Georgie's innocent?"

"Put it this way. I'm trying to find evidence that will demonstrate her innocence. I'll keep you up to date."

I returned to my car with a half-formed theory and absolutely no evidence to back it up. For a start off, I didn't know where on Sheffield Road Estate the Endicotts lived and I didn't want to ask Karen. She'd be tempted to warn Ambrose off. Without the address(es) I had no starting point, and even if I knew and confronted Ambrose, he was hardly likely to crumble under my cross-examination. I needed something more concrete.

Still, finding his and the Endicotts' address would be a start, and I knew exactly where to get it. The public library. My old chum Kim Aspinall would dig it out for me. With both addresses, I could judge how closely they lived to each other.

Easy peasy. Unlike her partner, the supercilious and stuffy Alden Upley, Kim didn't mind breaking the odd rule for a friend and a couple of phone calls later, I had numbers 18 and 22 Throstle Mount. A further fifteen minutes spent following the satnav and I was parked further along street from the two addresses.

They were two-storey buildings, upper and lower flats, and because they were numbered bottom, top, bottom top, both addresses were on the ground floor, right next to each other with no more than a small fence separating them.

There was nothing significant about it except that their locations would mean they had a good idea of each other's comings and goings, and if the general, negative impression of Annie Endicott was right, she was probably a nosy parker who had (perhaps) challenged Ambrose on his behaviour at some time.

Scratch that. It meant that Ambrose was lying when he told me he barely knew the woman. That was like me saying I hardly knew Hazel McQuarrie or Barbara Timmins. I could write the weekly or even daily schedule of both my neighbours and I guessed Annie was of the same bent.

So where did such a deduction take me? Shenanigans with Heidi Flanagan, and the same with

Georgie and Karen, that's where, and I would bet that Annie knew about them.

The scenario drew itself in my head. She knew, she was slagging him off, she maybe even tried to blackmail him, and he decided to take executioner's action. (Note: 'executioner' not 'executive'.)

I was so busy running the various ideas through my tired mind that it took some time for me to register the yellow, 'scene of crime tape' across the door of number 24, and even when I registered it, it took a phone call to Mandy to confirm my immediate suspicion.

"Heidi Flanagan's address?"

"Twenty-four Throstle Mount. It's on Sheffield Road estate," she replied. "Why?"

"I'm sat almost outside the place right now. The Endicott's lived below her, at number 22, and Ambrose lived next door, at number 18. Mandy, that man has told me more lies in a couple of days than I can tell Dennis in a month."

"Well, it's not like we didn't already know their addresses, but even so, it proves nothing, Chrissy."

"As far as I'm concerned, it proves Ambrose knew both Annie and Heidi a darn sight better than he had admitted to me the other night. I think it's time I paid him another visit."

"Well, you just watch your step. If you're right, he's already got rid of Annie and Heidi, and he won't hesitate to deal with you in the same way."

"Forewarned is forearmed," I reminded her.

"Chucking clichés at me won't stop him braining you. Just be careful."

A check on the dashboard clock told me I was

getting later and later for picking up Cappy the Cat, but I asked myself when was life any different when I was on a case, and the answer was… never.

For the second time that day, I drove out to Haxford Health Spa, but this time I was looking for Jonathan Ambrose.

The young woman on reception couldn't help. "I'm sorry, but I haven't seen him all day. In fact, we had to put another trainer in on his last class."

"He hasn't rung in sick?"

She looked down her nose at me. "I'm not allowed to give out that kind of information. It's confidential."

"I appreciate that, but…" I struggled for a moment to think of a suitable excuse. "I think he might be in some danger."

I couldn't tell whether it was real shock registering on her face or a competent bit of acting, but it did the trick. "Between you me and the gatepost, no, he hasn't rung in. Mr Leeming was asking after him earlier on."

"Thank you."

Coming out of the spa, I climbed into my car again, and rang Karen. "I'm ringing about Jonathan. He hasn't turned into work."

"Not unusual. Especially after a few snifters last night."

"Oh. Would he be at your place then?"

"No. He didn't stay with me last night. He said he had some business to attend to, so he stayed home. Do you think something's happened to him, Christine?"

It was the first hint that she was worried and I

hastened to reassure her. "There's no reason to think anything of the kind, Karen. And you've just said it's not unusual for him to duck work now and then."

"Well, all I can tell you is he should be at home. I'll give him a bell."

"While you're doing that, I'll make my way there. I need a quick word with him."

I rang off, started the engine, and drove back to Sheffield Road Estate, weaved my way through the various streets, and into Throstle Mount, cruised up to the gate, stopped, climbed out, and strolled along the path to knock on the door of number eighteen. No answer.

"Who's tha looking for?"

I wouldn't have recognised the wizened features, but I recognised the voice and the thick Yorkshire accent. "Is it Mr Endicott?"

"Who's asking?"

"Christine Capper."

"By, tha's a nosy ha'pporth, int tha?"

"I get paid to be a nosy ha'pporth, Mr Endicott. I'm trying to get in touch with Jonathan Ambrose, and I know he lives here. Have you seen anything of him?"

"Nay, lass. I've been working all day, haven't I? Aye, and I'd better get back to it else I'll have that slimy git, Lecher Fleecing on me back."

I gave him a grudging half smile, then made my way to the back of the building, where I knew that the ground floor flats had a rear door. That was locked, as was the side entrance. From there, I stepped into the small front garden, pressed my face to the window and looked in.

I recoiled instantly. I don't know whether it was Ambrose or someone else, but there was a man, lying face down in front of the fireplace, and what looked like a pool of blood gathered around his head.

Chapter Twenty-Two

When the police arrived, I was sat in my car, still shaking. My mind was flooded with memories of the Prater case and my discovery of a retired police officer who had been killed in a similar manner to Ambrose, the difference being, that the cop had his neck broken, whereas in this case, once Paddy and Mandy had checked Ambrose, they confirmed that a) it was him and b) he had been beaten to death to such a degree that he had bled all over the carpet.

Paddy was in a mean mood, and unwilling to tolerate my shattered nerves when he got into the passenger seat of my Renault.

"First question, what were you doing round here?"

"I needed to speak to him, I couldn't get an answer."

"When are you gonna learn to mind your own bloody business?"

I could feel my temper rising. "People pay me not to mind my own blinking business, Paddy. Right now you've got my client walled up for something she didn't do."

"You don't know that. For your inf—"

I cut him off. "I do know it. First Annie Endicott, then Heidi Flanagan, now Jonathan Ambrose. Two people who live so closely together, they could touch hands over the fence. I don't care about the different MO's, the three deaths are all linked, and since you've got Georgie in custody, she can't possibly have murdered Ambrose. It's obvious that someone else did, and if that's the case, then someone else killed all three of them."

"Which just shows how much you know, smartarse."

I delivered my most thunderous glare. "What are you talking about?"

"Forensics found traces of monkswood in Tibbett's garage, the place where she makes up the diet shakes. She poisoned the Endicott woman. Obviously, she didn't smash Ambrose's brains to bits, but she could just as easily have done Flanagan." He prepared to get out of the car. "I'll send Sonny Scott to take your statement. When he's done, clear off home, and don't get under my feet again."

"In that case, keep your feet out of my way." He climbed out and I shouted after him, "And it's monkshood, not monkswood, you dipstick."

I realised it was pointless trying to get any sense out of him, so after Sonny took my statement, I started the engine and drove for home in a fit of despondency edged with anger, the latter directed at Paddy Quinn.

Finding traces of monkshood in Georgie's garage was easy to explain... well, not easy but not hard either. It depended on whether the real killer (I really was still convinced of Georgie's innocence) could get access to the garage, and given Georgie's lackadaisical attitude to everything, it probably would not be that difficult.

The real problem now was the same as it had always been. Who?

There were any number of scenarios. Ambrose could have murdered Annie and planted those traces. Endicott had even better opportunity considering he did Georgie's gardening work. And I couldn't rule out Karen. Yes, she sounded sympathetic towards her sister, but that could have been a front. But in the case of Endicott or Karen, what was the motive for killing Annie, Ambrose, and Heidi?

Sex reared its ugly head right away. Ambrose had given Annie the dubious benefits of his fitness, so Walt murdered his wife. Heidi knew and threatened to shop him, so he killed her, and next door neighbour Ambrose deserved his fate because he'd lured Annie to his bed. But in that case, why didn't Endicott kill Ambrose before Heidi? Because Ambrose had been staying with Karen and today was the first opportunity Endicott had.

The theory wasn't bad, but fell apart at the first hurdle. I had never met or even seen a photograph of Annie, but based on others' opinions, she didn't sound like the type for bedhopping, and if she was anywhere near Endicott's age, she was way older than Ambrose.

That aside, it was noticeable that Endicott had avoided me since Annie's murder. A brief telephone conversation with him on Thursday, and a slightly acerbic one to one when I was looking for Ambrose, but I'd never been able to pin him down for a proper grilling. Where would I find him now? As a peripatetic gardener, he could be anywhere in the Haxford area.

I called at Breakfast to Bedtime on Moor Road and picked up a box of Kipling cakes for Hazel McQuarrie as a thank you for looking after Cappy the Cat, and I was turning into Bracken Close when I recalled Endicott's final words. "I'd better get back to it else I'll have that slimy git, Lecher Leeming on me back." He was at Haxford Health Spa.

I nosed the car slowly into the drive and parked alongside Barry's van. Time for a bite and a brew. I could tackle Walton Endicott later.

First, I paid a quick call to Hazel and asked if she could cope with our moody moggie for the rest of the afternoon because I would have to go out again.

"I keep telling you, Chrissy, it's no problem, you get on and do what you have to. Cappy's quite content with me.

The look on my pet pussy's face told a different story as I escaped again, and hurried round home to find dustsheets spread over the kitchen floor and Barry Snodgrass busy rolling paint onto the ceiling.

"Watch you don't get splashes on your shoes, Christine," he warned me.

Too late. I'd already trodden in a splotch of paint on one of the sheets.

He chuckled at my unladylike language. "That's why I always wear me short wellies when I'm painting. If I took any home and walked it into the carpet, our lass'd go bananas."

I know how she felt, I thought as I switched on the kettle. "Want a cuppa, Barry?"

"Sounds like a plan."

I took off my trainers, made my way to the bedroom where I put on my slippers and then came back, made tea for him and me, and took mine into the conservatory. I also took my trainers, a wet rag and some cleaning materials.

Fortunately the paint was still wet-ish and it didn't take much of an effort to get it off. I vowed that I would come and go via the conservatory exit and the side path until he was finished.

He'd made quite a bit of progress during my absence. The tiling was done and although the cooker was still pulled forward, I guessed it would not be long before the tile cement was solid enough to let me use the appliance.

Barry confirmed it when I popped back into the kitchen to tell him I had to go out again.

"By the time you get back, your stove will be back where it belongs, your ceiling will be done and you're right to use all your kitchen tackle." He drank from his beaker. "So, where are you going at this hour on a Friday? Anywhere exciting?"

"Haxford Health Spa."

"Ah. Fletcher Leeming's empire. Trying to get a bit of weight off, are you?"

I counted silently to five. If I didn't need my kitchen done, Mr Snodgrass would be close to summary execution. "No. It's a case I'm working on."

"I was just gonna say you don't look as if you need to lose weight."

That's the way to do it, Mr Snodgrass, I thought. Crawl back into my good books. Especially if you're hoping to get the job of redecorating the front room before Christmas.

"You do know I'm a private investigator?"

"Aye. Dennis said summat about it once over. And I've heard you mention it on the wireless. I think you mentioned it t'other day, too. Good fun, is it?"

"My radio work can be fun, but working as a private eye is frustrating. You've heard about Annie Endicott's murder?" I waited for him to nod. "Well, I'm trying to prove that the woman the police have in custody is innocent. I think it was Annie's husband."

He laughed. "Old Wally? He's a noughty old gripe, but I can't see him snuffing Annie out. She was a tough old boot, you know. In a straight scrap between Annie and Wally, she'd have won by a knockout."

But not if he poisoned her first, I thought. I changed the subject. "Do you know Fletcher Leeming?"

He nodded. "Asked me to quote for painting a few rooms and when I gave him a price, he asked how big a discount for cash. I told him I don't work for big concerns like that on a cash basis. Strictly through the books. I don't mind with householders like you, but not big companies. See, if owt happens, like a tax audit or summat, they can drop you into all sorts of trouble. You must know what I mean. Your Dennis does work for the cops doesn't he, but it's always on account, never cash. Anyway, Leeming never came back to me and the last I heard it was some one man band from Huddersfield that got the job."

"It's a curious way for any big concern to behave,

though, isn't it?" I said. "I mean the spa is owned by a national company, isn't it? Worth millions if not billions. Why would they try to save a few pounds or cut the VAT off a price?"

"It didn't make sense to me either, luv. For all I know, Leeming was shoving the cash in his back pocket. I don't know and I don't really care. It's not how I work."

I was with him on that point, but it did raise the ghost of suspicion somewhere at the back of my mind. I dismissed it. I was not commissioned to investigate possible, minor fraud committed by Fletcher Leeming.

In order to distract my agile mind, I looked at Barry's half wellington boots. Where wellies usually came up to the calf, these reached just above the ankles, and he had his white overalls tucked into them. Dark grey, they were splashed with coloured paint from across the spectrum and gave the impression of Joseph's Amazing Technicolor Dream-Boots

"They're quite neat, aren't they," I said.

He took off the left boot so I could see it better. I could have lived without it but he seemed determined to 'sell' me on them. "Sixty quid, retail, good for soaking up the splashes, easy on your feet and easy to get on and off before and after a day's work." He bent the toe upwards to demonstrated its pliability, and then put the boot back on. "And like I say, they keep the missus happy.

He pulled the boot up tight and tucked the overall bottoms in... but not before I noticed the crease they created in his overalls, like a tiny, almost invisible line around the point where they gripped his lower leg. Where had I seen that before?

In my mind's eye, I ran through a series of images of the people I had encountered over the last few days: Georgie Tibbett, Val Wharrier, Fletcher Leeming, Karen Dawkins, Jonathan Ambrose, Heidi Flanagan, Patricia Keenan, Walton Endicott. One of them had those same creases.

And then it appeared, and along with it came a slight correction. Walton Endicott didn't say Lecher Leeming. He said, Lecher *Fleecing*, and with that, I suddenly understood everything.

"I'm sorry, Barry, but I'm going to have to leave. If you're done before I get back, just drop the door on the latch. Dennis and I both have our keys."

"Sure thing. And I'll see you tomorrow if not before."

I jammed my damp trainers back on my feet, hurried through the conservatory exit, along the side of the house and almost leapt into the car.

We'd all been wrong all along. Well, nobody did that to Christine Capper. I didn't do confrontations but there were times when…

Hang on. This person had already poisoned one woman, and battered two others, one a fitness trainer to death. And I was going into a head to head?

I took to my phone and rang Paddy.

"Haven't I told you often enough to sod off and mind your own business?"

"Yes, but, Paddy…"

He cut the call. I sat there fuming for a good few minutes. The man was an imbecile, but one with the power to ignore others. What was I supposed to do?

Go charging in like the Light Brigade and succumb to the cannon fire?

Sucking in a deep breath, I rang Mandy.

"Chrissy, I've got Paddy here calling you so many names that I don't think I've ever heard some of them."

"I know. And you've got it wrong, Mandy. You and him and me. We all have. I know what's going on and I think I know why. Get Paddy down to Haxford Health Spa and I'll meet you there. I need a quick word with someone and from there we'll have your killer."

"If you've got this wrong—"

"Then it's my backside Paddy will kick, but I don't want to face this nutter alone. Be there."

With that, I rang off, and pulled out of the drive for the fifteen-minute journey to either success or personal humiliation.

Chapter Twenty-Three

Haxford Health Spa appeared ahead, and I was engulfed with mixed emotions. Anger on the one hand, the familiar wrath I felt whenever I confronted someone who had needlessly taken another's life. It was mixed with trepidation. If I was right – and I was fully convinced of it – this was a very dangerous man. If Mandy and/or Paddy did not show up, would I be wise to confront him? The sensible answer was, 'no', but I didn't always deploy sense in such situations.

I parked the car, looked around and spotted Walt Endicott plodding along behind a petrol mower while working on the vast expanse of grass surrounding the buildings.

I switched off the engine, climbed out of the car, locked it up, and made my way across the grass to join him. He was wearing ear protectors, and he didn't hear me approach. Consequently, when I tapped him on the shoulder he almost jumped out of his skin. He turned to face me, his face livid.

"What's tha doing sneaking up on folk like that?"

"I'm sorry. I didn't mean to startle you."

He tapped the ear protectors, turned back to his machine and switched it off, then removed the headset. "What did tha say?"

"I said, I'm sorry. I didn't mean to startle you. I need to ask you a couple of questions, Mr Endicott."

"Does tha think I've nowt better to do than talk to the likes of you."

"It's important. Earlier today, when I was trying to find Jonathan Ambrose, you referred to Fletcher Leeming as, quote, Lecher Fleecing. I understand Lecher. A friend of mine explained it to me. But why Fleecing?"

"Cos that's what he does. Half these silly sods paying for the rooms are handing over cash, and it goes straight in his pocket. Yet, folk like me, doing a proper job on the grounds, has to invoice him, and wait owt up to two months for me money."

It was as I suspected. "He's taking the money for himself? You know that for a fact, do you, Mr Endicott?"

"Aye. I do. I were working here late one night last summer, and I'd seen him going round, collecting the cash here and there, and then I spotted him sitting in his car. He were counting money. And then, he stuck a big chunk of it in his glove box, counted out the rest, put it back in his pocket, and went back into the building."

It called to mind what I had seen on Tuesday evening outside the Barley Mow, when he was in his car. Did he lean over and drop something into his glove box? Quite possibly. As evidence, it would hardly stand up in court. Leeming would simply claim that he had a legitimate, company expense to pay in cash. It would need more than mine or Endicott's say-so..

"Did you ever mention this to your wife, Mr

Endicott?"

"I did. When she told me she were joining that diet group and she'd be coming here. I told her, I said, you ought to keep away from there, lass. Course, she took no notice."

"Would your wife have mentioned this to Heidi Flanagan?"

"As a matter of fact, I think she did. Our Annie didn't like Flanagan, and when she stopped going to this silly bloody diet club, she told Flanagan that the money she was handing over to the Tibbett woman was going straight into Leeming's pocket. She was like that, Annie. Anything to put one over on people she didn't like."

My suspicions began to mesh, and this information coupled with the lies Jonathan Ambrose told me concerning his non-existent (according to him) liaison with Heidi Flanagan, explained just about everything.

Endicott's irritation was beginning to get the better of him again. "What's all this about?"

Was it wise to tell him? Wisdom, they say, comes with age, and I wasn't old enough yet. "It'll be very difficult to prove, Mr Endicott, but I think Leeming murdered your wife."

He glared at the building, threw down his ear protectors, and was about to march over there when I stopped him.

"The police are on their way. Don't do anything rash."

"Rash? I'll smash his bloody brains in, that's what I'll do."

"No, Mr Endicott. Please. I've absolutely no

proof. It's only a suspicion."

"Aye, well, if I have to, I'll beat it out of him."

"For the last time, Mr Endicott, stay there. Let me confront him. That's what I'm being paid for."

The sense of my words got through to him, and I made my way to the building (with Endicott following slowly behind), walked up to reception, and asked to see him.

"I'm not sure if he's available, Mrs Capper. Hold on a moment." She picked up the phone, muttered into it, and then said, "Yes, He'll see you. You know where his office is."

I nodded and made my way through the double doors into the building proper. Once there, I paused, took out my smartphone, and set up the voice recorder. With it going, I knocked on Leeming's door, waited for his invitation, and walked in.

He greeted me genially, waved me to the seat opposite, and as I sat down, he asked, "So what can I do for you this time, Mrs Capper?"

With the phone resting on my lap, praying that it would pick up the conversation, I said, "You can admit what you've done, Mr Leeming."

A frown crossed his clear brow. "I'm sorry? I don't think I understand."

"Oh, I'm sure you do. You poisoned Annie Endicott, you beat Heidi Flanagan to death, and earlier today, you beat Jonathan Ambrose to death, too. And all to stop them exposing you for stealing money that rightly belonged to the spa." I gave him a cruel smile. "Money from the people who paid in cash. How did you work it, Mr Leeming? Fifty percent to you, fifty percent to your employers?"

He fell into a stunned silence which probably lasted up to a minute, then said, "I'm sure I don't know what you're talking about."

"I think you do. You were seen, Mr Leeming, sitting in your car, putting money to one side. What happened? Did Annie Endicott threaten to expose you? I mean, let's face it, she was that kind of woman. Did she ask you for a cut? And Endicott himself told you about the monkshood, didn't he? I think you went along to see her, she let you in, thinking that you're going to pay her, and you managed to drop the aconite into her diet shake. Obviously, she would have noticed it the moment she took a drink, but for a man like you, that would be easy to handle, wouldn't it? Pinch her nose and force her to swallow the rest. But she'd already told Heidi Flanagan, and I guess Heidi wanted a piece of the action? I saw you both outside the Barley Mow on Tuesday evening and I wondered why she was all smiles with you. I thought you were having an affair, but she was actually asking for a payoff, wasn't she? And, considering she had slept with Ambrose, she told him about it, and he asked for a cut too, didn't he? Everyone knows he was always short of money. Heidi was easy, but Ambrose was a more difficult prospect. How would you tackle a fitness fanatic like him? Simple: you hit him from behind, didn't you?" I smiled again. "Tell me how much I've got wrong?"

The silence was shorter this time and he broke it with a soft chuckle. "Quite a bit, actually. I mean, you are right. I did kill all three of them. But it wasn't quite as simple as you said. Endicott gave me the idea when he complained about the monkshood. A few days before that, his wife, as you so rightly assumed, came to me, told me what she knew and demanded a percentage. I asked her to give me a little time, and she did. What you didn't know, indeed, what she didn't know, was my, er, occasional meetings with Georgie Tibbett at her place, and more intimate dates with Flanagan. You were right about that, too. I'd hardly call it an affair. More like the occasional connection. With Tibbett, our meetings were purely business, but Flanagan was, let's say, hard up for it. During one such meeting with Tibbett I had the opportunity to steal a key for her garage, and one Tuesday evening while she was railing at her diet group, I went along there, and made up a special shake containing monkshood. Not long after that, I went along to see Mrs Endicott, and left that shake with her. I knew she'd use it sooner or later. It gave it me a pleasant surprise when she drank it just a few days after I'd left it. Visiting Georgie's garage, also gave me the opportunity to leave traces of monkshood here and there. And you know something, Mrs Capper, Georgie is so lackadaisical that she didn't even realise one of her keys was missing." He laughed again. "The Flanagan woman was easy. We'd been sharing a bed on and off for some time, and when Annie was found dead, she put two and two together, much the same as you have done, and on Tuesday night she asked to see me, I went along to her place, she demanded a ridiculous five thousand pounds to keep her mouth shut. So I paid her off with a heavy walking stick." He waved to the corner of his office where the stick rested against the freestanding coat hook.

"And Ambrose?"

"Once again, you hit the nail on the head. Heidi Flanagan had told him, and when she died, he came knocking on the door. He didn't want a large payoff. He wanted a cut. Fifty-fifty. He even offered to help me collect the money every week. Once again, we couldn't do that kind of business here, so I arranged to meet him at his flat. There was some haggling, and eventually I agreed to his proposition, whereupon he turned his back, reached up to take a bottle of Scotch from a shelf so we could celebrate. A fatal mistake, Mrs Capper, as he learned when my walking stick caught him at the back of the head. A few more blows and it was goodbye Jonathan Ambrose."

I began to worry. He looked too confident, too sure of himself, and I'd heard nothing of any approaching police vehicles.

"By and large," he said, "you've done well. You put things together quite admirably, but there's one other item you missed."

I put on a fake show of calm. "And that was?"

"The part where I take a local radio presenter-cum-private investigator for a drive in my car, and only I come back." He got to his feet.

"I think you should be careful, Mr Leeming. The police know where I am, and they know why I'm here. Your receptionist will tell them that I checked in. How are you going to explain it if I suddenly disappear?"

"That won't be difficult, Madam. When I confess to the ending of our long-running affair, and of course, by the time the police do get here, your car will have disappeared along with you."

Did I mention a feeling of trepidation when I first arrived at the spa? Well it was no longer a problem. Right now, it was outright fear. This man was over a foot taller than me, and I didn't have even the most basic of weapons such as an umbrella.

I bolted for the door, my mobile phone dropping from my lap. Inevitably, I never made it. Leeming grabbed me by the arm, and while he held on, he reached down, picked up the phone, studied the screen, shut down the recorder and dropped the phone in his pocket.

"Clever," he said. "Sadly, no one will ever hear it. They won't even find your phone."

He turned me to face him, and gripped both my arms so tight that it was painful. I tried kicking. A waste of effort. He was so tall, his arms so long, that I could neither connect with his knees never mind his more sensitive regions.

"Now, Mrs Capper. Here's what will happen. There is a rear exit to this building, and getting out through it will not be a problem. However, if you should try to scream or shout, I won't wait to drive you to Haxford reservoir. I will kill you there and then. Behave yourself, and you never know, your knight in shining armour, whether that be the police or some other nosy so-and-so, might just save your miserable, unworthy hide."

"You seriously think I'm going to go quietly, do you, Leeming? Walk away with you to my death? You have one more screw loose than I thought."

"It would be no problem for me to kill you here, and carry you out through the rear exit. If that's what you prefer, then so be it."

And his large hands reached for my throat. He squeezed, I struggled, I fought, I wriggled, I kicked out, but I knew it was a losing battle. It would not be long before I fell into unconsciousness and then eternity.

I'd almost resigned myself to it when I heard the sound of the office door opening, someone hurrying in, and then a loud thump. His grip relaxed, his hands fell away from my throat and he dropped to the carpet.

Walton Endicott glared down at him, and blessed darkness overcame me.

***

I don't know how long I was unconscious, but it couldn't have been more than a few minutes. When I came to, I was flat on my back, head tilted backwards to keep my airway open, the concerned faces of Walton Endicott, Mandy Hiscoe, Paddy Quinn looking down on me, and a first aider was taking my pulse.

I coughed and waved the first aider away before trying to sit up. My neck hurt, and the action made my head spin. I laid back down again.

"Leeming?"

I aimed the question at anyone who was willing to answer. Almost inevitably, it was Mandy who replied.

"Thanks to Mr Endicott, he's unconscious and has a sizeable bump on his head. And we got your phone out of his pocket."

I smiled at Endicott. "Thank you."

"Nay problem, lass. After what he did to my

missus and t'others, he's lucky I didn't top him."

"He's not worth going to prison for, Mr Endicott." I focused on Mandy. "I had the voice recorder on. I don't know how much use it'll be, but you might be able to enhance it. He told me everything."

Paddy took front and centre. "At least you're all right, Christine. Some nasty bruises around your neck, but you'll survive. Now tell me, is this going to convince you to keep your bloody nose out?"

I tried to smile and it hurt. "I don't think so, Paddy. Let's face it, if it wasn't for me, you wouldn't have anyone to complain about, would you?"

Epilogue

Eventually, Fletcher Leeming was charged and successfully prosecuted on three counts of murder. He received a mandatory life sentence with a tariff of thirty years, the minimum time he would spend in prison. The judge was not persuaded by his remorse, and in murdering his three victims, he had shown regard only for himself, and not them nor their right to life.

When he got home from work that evening and saw the damage Leeming had done to my neck, Dennis came down firmly in Paddy Quinn's court and barred me from any future investigations of this nature. Needless to say, I told him exactly what he could do with his ban.

Georgie Tibbett and Karen Dawkins were fully reconciled as sisters and business partners. The Haxford Losers Club and Haxford (not so) Heavies would be united as the Haxford Heavy Losers. It still didn't quite grab me as a sensible name for a diet group, but the last I heard, they were doing quite well, and about two months after the case was closed, the sisters appeared on Radio Haxford, the subject of one of Christine Capper's Interviews. A week or two after I interviewed them, I sat down with Tel Wheatley, and spent an enlightening hour discussing his sorry experience of failed ambitions and unseen, unheard racism.

Barry Snodgrass did a superb job on my kitchen and I treated him to a £50 bonus on top of his bill, much to Dennis's dismay.

Soon after the case was closed, we had a letter from Foulsham confirming that Eunice was the sole beneficiary in William Capper's estate, but it would be some months before we knew exactly what that meant. A further letter also told me that once I signed the agreement, they would be happy to add my name and credentials to their preferred investigators' list. I wasn't holding my breath for a flood of calls.

As for me, I learned a couple of valuable lessons from the episode, the first and most important of which was to avoid confrontations with very tall men who had hands the size of shovels.

I also learned something about jumping to conclusions. I'm quite skilled at it, but my maidenly, neo-Victorian attitude to matters carnal led me along an erroneous route, attributing everything to horizontal shenanigans of the extramarital kind, yet ultimately, this case had precious little to do with loose living men and women. It was all about financial greed.

And that's all for this week. Tune in again next week for more comings and goings in and around Haxford. For now, I'll bid you goodbye.

THE END

THANK YOU FOR READING. I HOPE YOU HAVE ENJOYED THIS BOOK. WOULD YOU BE KIND ENOUGH TO LEAVE A RATING OR REVIEW ON AMAZON?

The Author

David W Robinson retired from the rat race after the other rats objected to his participation, and he now lives with his long-suffering wife in sight of the Pennine Moors outside Manchester.

Best known as the creator of the light-hearted and ever-popular **Sanford 3rd Age Club Mysteries**, and in the same vein, **Mrs Capper's Casebook**. He also produces darker, more psychological crime thrillers as in the **Feyer & Drake** thrillers and occasional standalone titles.

He, produces his own videos, and can frequently be heard grumbling against the world on Facebook at **https://www.facebook.com/davidrobinsonwriter/** and has a YouTube channel at

By the same Author
Mrs Capper's Casebook

Christine Capper is a solid, down to earth Yorkshire
lass, witty, plain spoken, but with an innate sense of
inquiry (all right, then, she's nosy). She passes her
days in the West Yorkshire town of Haxford looking
after her long-suffering husband, Dennis, a man with
an obsession for all things automotive, and putting
him right when he goes wrong, which is more often
than not. She takes care of their pet, Cappy the Cat,
a feline with attitude, dotes on her granddaughter
Bethany, and is openly proud of her son, Simon, now
Acting Detective Constable Capper of the Haxford
force.

A former police officer, she's Haxford's only trained
and licenced private investigator. She's choosy about
the cases she takes on but appears destined to be
dragged into more serious affairs, during which she
passes on her findings to her friend, Detective
Sergeant Mandy Hiscoe and Mandy's immediate
boss, DI Paddy Quinn, a man who is quite open about
his dislike for private eyes.

A series of light-hearted mysteries, laced with Yorkshire grit and wit, Mrs Capper's Casebooks are exclusive to Amazon available for the Kindle and in paperback.

You can find them at:
https://mybook.to/cappseries

The Sanford 3rd Age Club Mysteries

These titles are published and managed by Darkstroke Books

A decade on from their debut, there are 26 volumes (soon to be 27) and a special in the Sanford 3rd Age Club Mystery series.

We follow the travels and trials of amateur sleuth Joe Murray and his two best friends, Sheila Riley and Brenda Jump. The short, irascible Joe, proprietor of The Lazy Luncheonette in Sanford, West Yorkshire, jollied along by the bubbly Brenda and Sheila, but only his friends, but also his employees, all three leading lights in the Sanford 3rd Age Club (STAC for short). And it seems that wherever they go on their outings on holidays in the company of the born-again teenagers of the 3rd Age Club, they bump into… MURDER.

A major series of whodunits marinated in Yorkshire humour, they are exclusive to Amazon and you can find them at: **https://mybook.to/stac**

Other Works

I also turn out darker works such as The Anagramist and The Frame with Chief Inspector Samantha Feyer and civilian consultant Wesley Drake, and the standalone The Cutter.

For details visit <u>https://dwrob.com/the-dark/</u>

Free Books

Like what you've seen so far? Why to subscribe to my newsletter? I guaranteed that you will not be inundated with emails, and your address will never be sold on. Once you sign up, you will receive details of to one but TWO free novellas.

For more information visit
<u>https://dwrob.com/readers-club/</u>

Printed in Great Britain
by Amazon